DINOSAUR DETECTIVE CLUB

BOOK #4

Raptor's Revenge

Mackinac Island Press

for the love of reading

Other PaleoJoe Books

Dinosaur Detective Club Chapter Books

#1 The Disappearance of Dinosaur Sue
#2 Stolen Stegosaurus
#3 Secret Sabertooth
#5 Mysterious Mammoths

Hidden Dinosaurs

...and more to come...

Text Copyright 2007 Joseph Kchodl
Illustration Copyright 2007 Mackinac Island Press, Inc.

First Edition

Library of Congress Cataloging-in-Publication Data on file

PaleoJoe's Dinosaur Detective Club #4 Raptor's Revenge

Summary: PaleoJoe and the Dinosaur Detective Club work to get a rare fossil in the museum, while following clues to solve mysterious happenings in the Raptor Room.

ISBN 978-1-934133-37-8

Fiction
10 9 8 7 6 5 4 3 2 1

Printed and bound in the United States by Cushing-Malloy, Inc.

A Mackinac Island Press, Inc. publication
Traverse City, Michigan

www.mackinacislandpress.com

*Dedicated to the imagination
and discovery that
all children have with dinosaurs.*

RAPTOR'S

REVENGE

TABLE OF CONTENTS

1. SILENT WATCHER 10
2. DINOSAUR GRASSHOPPER 12
3. TERROR IN THE BLUE CANVAS BAG . . 17
4. SABER DISCOVERS DANGER 22
5. SILENCE IN THE TOMBS 28
6. THE ART OF BARGING 33
7. SPECTER OF DOOM 39
8. SABOTAGE! 45
9. THE RAPTOR ROOM 49
10. A STINKY CLUE 56
11. SHADOWS AND SPIES 61
12. STOWAWAY 68
13. THE OUTLAW TRAIL 74
14. BONE RANCH 79
15. THE ANSWER IS NO 83
16. BUTCH 88
17. DINOSAUR NATIONAL MONUMENT . . 93

TABLE OF CONTENTS

18. DEAD MAN'S ROAD 99

19. A RAPTOR ENCOUNTER 103

20. OUT OF CONTROL ON
       DEAD MAN'S ROAD 108

21. CLEVELAND MAKES A DECISION . . 113

22. WHITE WATER 118

23. MIKE 124

24. KIDNAPPED 131

25. CALAMITY CANYON 136

26. THE CABIN OF BONES 140

27. BONE MINE 145

28. THE TRAP 151

29. THE BALBOA CURSE 155

30. SHELLY'S PLAN 160

31. THE VANDAL 166

32. GREED 172

33. THE TOMBS ONCE AGAIN 175

CHAPTER ONE

SILENT WATCHER

Across the street from the Balboa Museum of Natural History a man in dark sunglasses, hid in the shadowed doorway of a deserted shop. He was carefully watching the museum entrance. He seemed particularly interested in the strange behavior of a boy dressed in a neon green t-shirt who was jittering up and down the museum steps in an odd and peculiar way.

Taking a miniature, but powerful, pair of binoculars from his pocket, the man focused in on the boy. The kid was crouching on a step, concentrating on something on the ground at his feet. Whatever it was, it was invisible to the watcher. Then, suddenly, frog-like, the boy popped forward to scrabble on the ground with his hands.

The man frowned. He adjusted his binoculars bringing the face of the boy into sharp focus. The boy was someone the man recognized.

"Spike," he muttered. "What the devil are you up to?"

Just then the man spotted two figures mounting the steps to join the boy. Through the high magnification of his binoculars he could clearly see the features of the middle aged woman, her arms filled with books, and, jouncing along beside her, the red haired girl carrying a blue canvas bag slung over her shoulder.

The man gave a low, sinister laugh as he watched the group come together. Then, quickly concealing the binoculars in his pocket, he turned his collar up around his ears. A quick nervous glance from his hiding place showed the coast was clear. He left the shelter of the doorway. Moving fast and unnoticed, the man hurried away. Soon he was lost to sight.

CHAPTER TWO

DINOSAUR GRASSHOPPER

"Dakota Jackson, what on earth?" Shelly Brooks bounced up the steps of the Balboa Museum to where the boy in the neon green t-shirt was sprawled flat on his stomach.

"Hi, Shelly!" Dakota rolled over onto his back looking up at his red-haired friend. "I can see up your nose!"

Shelly roughly prodded him in the side with one pink high-top sneaker. "Nice. Now, get up, bean brain, you look awfully silly on your back on the museum steps."

Awkwardly Dakota got to his feet. He kept his hands cupped to his chest as though he held something captive. As he struggled to stand, Shelly was joined by her Gamma Brooks.

"Hi, Mrs. Brooks," Dakota greeted Shelly's grandmother.

"Hi yourself, young man," Gamma Brooks puffed a bit from her climb up the steps. Her arms, as usual, were full of books. Dakota didn't know anyone who read quite so much as Gamma Brooks. "What do you have in your hands?" she asked.

"Oh!" said Dakota excitedly. "It's the coolest thing! I caught this grasshopper see and..."

"A *grasshopper*!!?" Shelly rolled her eyes and brushed by him. "In case you haven't noticed, genius, grasshoppers are about as common around here as stones!"

"But, wait!" Dakota hopped up the steps to block her path waving his clasped hands under her nose. "There is something really different about this grasshopper."

"What, it can recite the alphabet backwards?"

"Yes, I recognize sarcasm when I hear it," said Dakota. "But I'm telling you there is something cool and strange about this insect."

Shelly snorted.

"Well, really," Gamma Brooks interrupted. "Some grasshoppers are very interesting, Shellypop. Very unique."

"Right," said Dakota eagerly. "Unique. Exactly. This grasshopper is unique!" He wasn't really sure what 'unique' meant but he was sure that if Gamma

13

Brooks said it, it was a smart thing to say.

"Well, let's see it then," said Shelly.

Carefully Dakota separated his fingers just the tiniest bit so that Shelly could see. Shelly leaned close and...

The grasshopper escaped!

Quick as lightning the insect wriggled from Dakota's grasp, whirred into a giant leap, and landed *plop* on the top of Shelly's head.

"Oops," said Dakota.

"Oh, hairy grasshoppers!" squealed Shelly. "Get it off!"

Normally, Shelly was not even the least bit squeamish. In fact she didn't mind worms, or snakes or even spiders. But she did not–as you would not–enjoy anything that sprang at her without warning to land *plop* on her head–no matter what it was.

But before anyone could do anything, Shelly, in her panic, grabbed a book from Gamma Brooks and whacked it on her own head perhaps a little harder than she had planned.

SMAP!

"Ouch!" Shelly cried. Then her eyes went wide in horror and she turned to look at Dakota. "Oh, *eeeewwwww!* Dakota, do I have–*grasshopper guts* in my hair?"

But Dakota was no help. With both hands clamped tightly over his mouth, he was slowly turning purple, as he tried not to laugh at Shelly.

"Oh, oh, oh, oh...." Shelly grimaced as she gingerly reached up to feel the top of her head.

"Relax, Shellypebble," said Gamma Brooks. "There is no smashed grasshopper on your head. He jumped off just in time and look!" She held up a small, clear plastic container. "I caught him!"

My grandmother is always prepared, thought Shelly rubbing her sore head. Gamma Brooks was an amateur entomologist. An entomologist was a scientist that studied insects. And a scientist that studied insects would always be prepared to capture the odd or interesting specimen that might hop or wiggle their way.

Dakota took in a large gulp of air and let out a whoop of laughter. "I never thought I'd see the day when Shelly Brooks hit herself over her own head!" he gasped and, still laughing, stooped to gather up the

books Gamma had dropped when she captured the grasshopper.

Shelly scowled. This sort of thing only happened to her when she was around Dakota, so really it was all his fault.

"You should have seen your face!" he crowed.

Shelly stuck her tongue out at him.

"Oh my," said Gamma Brooks closely examining the insect. "Dakota, your little friend here is a *Tropidolophus formosus,* a dinosaur grasshopper."

"What!?" exclaimed Shelly and Dakota together.

"Yes," said Gamma Brooks. "There's no mistake. But there is something very strange about this."

"You mean besides Shelly attempting to brain herself with a book?" asked Dakota smothering another laugh.

"What is it, Gamma?" asked Shelly elbowing him in the side.

"It's that *Tropidolophus formosus* is not found in our state."

"Then," said Dakota, "how did he get here?"

CHAPTER THREE

TERROR IN THE BLUE CANVAS BAG

Everyone leaned closer to study the pale green grasshopper in Gamma Brook's plastic container.

"He's quite a handsome fellow, isn't he?" said Gamma.

"I like the brown spots on his back," said Dakota.

"Is it that crest thing on his head that makes people call him a dinosaur grasshopper?" asked Shelly.

"Exactly right, Puppypop," said Gamma Brooks with a big smile, using one of her odder terms of endearment. "It makes him look like a miniature *Dimetrodon*. You know, the sail-backed dinosaur."

17

"Yes, I know the one," said Shelly. "There's a skeleton of one on the second floor of the museum."

"So, where do you find grasshoppers like this?" asked Dakota.

"Yes," said Gamma Brooks and she squinted thoughtfully at their catch. "That is the question, isn't it? These grasshoppers are found in the west. As I remember it, their range is from Arizona to Wyoming and then east to Kansas, Oklahoma and Texas."

"So they are not found around here then?" asked Shelly.

"Not usually," said Gamma. "Well, I think I'll just take this little fellow inside with me. I'll put him on display today for visitors to the entomology room." And so, with the plastic container balanced carefully on her stack of books, Gamma Brooks made her way happily up the museum steps, disappearing through the doors at the top.

"Wait, Shelly," said Dakota as Shelly started up the steps after her grandmother.

"Now what, Dakota?" Shelly turned impatiently. She fully expected Dakota to start teasing her again about hitting herself on the head and so she was surprised to see a thoughtful look on his face.

"That grasshopper shouldn't be here," said Dakota.

"Yeah? So what?" Shelly shrugged. "Once I read about frogs raining from the sky. That shouldn't have happened either. Get used to it, Dakota. Bizarre things happen. I mean look at you!" Shelly couldn't resist but Dakota, amazingly, did not rise to the bait.

"Funny, Shelly. But seriously, I think there is something important about that grasshopper being here. I think we should investigate."

"The only thing around here that needs investigation, Dakota Jackson, is your intelligence. Come on. We're late for our meeting with PaleoJoe."

Dakota rolled his eyes. Leave it to Shelly to dismiss the one interesting thing to happen all week. Unfortunately, however, she was right as usual in one thing. They were late for their meeting with PaleoJoe. But as Dakota began to follow Shelly up the steps of the Balboa Museum, the blue canvas bag Shelly had slung over her shoulder suddenly caught his attention. As he watched it bounce gently against Shelly's hip his eyes grew wide in surprise.

The bag was moving on its own! The blue canvas sides were bulging here and there, as though some sort of something alive was punching out the sides of it.

"Shelly!" Dakota yelled. "Your bag is alive!"

Shelly stopped, looked back at the wide-eyed Dakota, and shook her head in pity. "Poor boy," she said. "Of course my bag is not alive."

"But I saw it move," Dakota insisted.

"Well, of course it moved," Shelly came back down the steps to stand beside Dakota. "But it isn't my bag that's alive. It's what is *in* my bag that's alive."

"Is it a snake?" asked Dakota hopefully. Dakota

had a thing about snakes. He liked them.

"Nope," Shelly shook her head mysteriously. "Do you want to see?"

"Do I want to see? Does chocolate melt in the sun? Of course I want to see!"

"Well, I guess it might be okay," said Shelly mysteriously. "I can give you just a peek but be very careful. There is a certain amount of danger involved here."

Trying hard not to laugh at the serious look on Dakota's face, Shelly carefully opened her bag just a crack. The sides bulged and Dakota leaned cautiously forward for a look.

"**ROAR!!**" yelled Shelly as loud as she could just as a small, whiskered brown striped head poked out of the bag.

And the effect was everything she could have hoped for.

Startled by her yell, Dakota reeled back, eyes wide and his mouth in a fishlike *O*. And then his foot slipped and, in order to prevent himself from falling down the steps, he windmilled his arms and did a sort of jiggly jump down the stairs backward, looking like a puppet suddenly cut from its strings.

Shelly reached out a hand to grab his arm, but she was laughing so hard that she too, lost her balance. So, somehow managing to stay on their feet, together they bumped and danced to the bottom of the stairs.

"Oh, oh," Shelly gasped and sat down on the

bottom step rocking to catch her breath. "Yikes!" Dakota tumbled beside her his teeth jarring a bit as he sat down on the cement step. "Was that necessary?" "Yes!" Shelly rocked back and forth with laughter.

"At least we've established my extraordinary ability to keep on my feet, even on the most dangerous of museum steps," said Dakota smugly. "Now, let's have a look in that bag of yours."

He reached over for Shelly's bag and carefully opened it. Reaching inside he scooped out the roaring terror of the blue canvas bag.

CHAPTER FOUR

SABER DISCOVERS DANGER

"His name is Saber," said Shelly reaching over to tickle under the creamy white chin of the small cat Dakota held in his hands. "He needs a home."

"*Merrow*," said Saber in a rough, growly voice that sounded twice as big as his small cat self. He looked seriously at Dakota out of amber eyes, flicked one stripy ear and completely stole Dakota's heart.

Dakota happily settled the chubby striped cat onto his knee. Hooking and unhooking small, barbed claws into Dakota's jeans, the small cat blinked lazily at Shelly and Dakota. While not quite a kitten, the cat was young and was about the size of a small, fat loaf of bread. He had a brown and white face with well-defined darker black stripes on his shoulders and sides. Dakota ran his fingers under Saber's chin and the cat, narrowing his honey yellow eyes to slits, began to purr in a rumble that sounded like miniature thunder.

"He certainly seems to like you," said Shelly smiling.

There was something a little different about this cat though. It was something that Dakota had noticed right away. Saber did not have a tail like normal cats. Instead he had a little stump. He looked like a small bobcat.

"What happened to his tail?" Dakota asked.

"Nothing happened to his tail," said Shelly. "It's the kind of breed he is. The vet called him an American Bobtail cat."

"That's why you call him Saber, isn't it?" asked Dakota catching on at once. "He's like the saber-toothed cats."

"Yep," said Shelly petting Saber along his stripy back. "He's a miniature saber-toothed cat."

Just recently Shelly and Dakota had gone on an adventure to La Brea where they had learned about the saber-toothed cats that had been trapped in the tar pits during the Pleistocene Era. In their investigation, Shelly and Dakota had discovered that these ferocious predators called *Smilodon* were a little shorter than modern lions, but about twice as heavy, and that they had bobtails.

23

"So what are you carrying him around for?" asked Dakota.

"Gamma is not allowed to have animals in her apartment," explained Shelly. "Saber needs to find a home and I don't want to take him to the Animal Shelter."

"He's not a kitten exactly," said Dakota, as Saber stepped off Dakota's knee to stretch his short furry length along the warm cement step.

"No, the vet said he is a young cat, like a teenager," said Shelly. "I found him in the alley in back of Gamma's apartment. We advertised, but no one has claimed him. I was hoping PaleoJoe might take him."

"I wish I could take him," said Dakota petting Saber's warm fur, "but I don't think my mom would let me."

"You could ask her though," said Shelly.

Dakota held the rumbling, soft cat to his cheek and received a rough-tongued lick on his ear.

"In the meantime," said Shelly, "it's back into the bag with you, Saber. We are late for our Dinosaur Detective Club meeting."

Shelly held open the bag and Dakota attempted to put Saber into it. Saber appeared willing enough to return to his temporary home but, just at that moment, a small ground squirrel scurried across the sidewalk capturing Saber's full attention and all his saber-toothed instinct as well.

Dakota tried to hold him, but it was like trying to hang onto smoke. With an agile twist, Saber was free and racing along the sidewalk after the small rodent.

"Dakota, do something!" Shelly shrieked beside him. "He's heading for the street!"

Horrified, Dakota saw that was indeed where Saber was heading. Cars swished by on the busy street. None would see or stop for a dashing cat. Tragedy was close.

Thinking quickly, Dakota grabbed Shelly's blue canvas bag and slung it into the path of the charging cat. Startled, Saber swerved and, at the last second, instead of running into the street he launched himself into the back of a pickup truck standing beside an expired parking meter.

Shelly, eyes wide, let out a small gasp. "That was close!"

"I'll get him," said Dakota.

25

Keeping one eye out for the possible return of the owner, Dakota approached the back end of the truck. It was a green beat up truck covered with mud and rust. The tailgate was missing. The bed was filled with dirt and grass. There were tools lashed down near the back of the cab. The window of the cab was opened. Dakota could see Saber inside the cab peeking out. It almost looked like he was smiling, thought Dakota.

"*Miirow*," Saber informed Dakota, looking intelligently at a fly that seemed to be caught in the cab as well.

"Saber," scolded Dakota. "That isn't your truck you know. "

"*Rarw,*" Saber seemed to agree as though this was obvious to anyone. Young cats, no matter how handsome their stripes, could not drive large green pickup trucks all the way from...

Dakota peered at the mud splattered license plate. "Arizona?" Dakota said in surprise as he read the state of the license plate.

"*Mmeew,*" Saber trilled and made a swat at the fly, which discovered the opening of the window and escaped.

Quickly, Dakota produced a small black notebook from his hip pocket. This was his Detective Notebook. He used it to record various important details. Rapidly he flipped through pages with headings such as *Important Rules,* or *Things to Do,* until he came to a page headed *Strange But Possibly Important Random*

Facts. Using a small pencil he copied the license plate number down.

"This is all very suspicious," he muttered as he clambered into the bed of the truck to get Saber. "Come here, Saber," he coaxed and gave a whispery whistle. But it appeared Saber was more than ready to return to Dakota. Scampering out the window, the small cat thumped down beside Dakota and demonstrated his ability to twine around ankles.

"Very nice," Dakota told him and reached down to pick him up. A light breeze swirled through the air and that's when Dakota got a whiff of the interior of the pickup's cab. And what he smelled was a smell that Dakota would never forget.

An old gym shoe smell.

One that still gave him nightmares.

"Come on, Saber," he said scooping the cat into his arms. "We need to get out of here, now!"

CHAPTER FIVE

SILENCE IN THE TOMBS

"I'm telling you, Shelly, this is important!" Dakota had to hop it to keep up with Shelly as she charged up the museum steps. "First there was the grasshopper, still alive by the way, and then the truck from Arizona and then that smell! I will never forget that smell. You really should pay attention to these things."

Saber was once more stowed safely in his blue canvas bag and Shelly was in full steam heading for PaleoJoe.

"I'll leave that to you, Dakota," she said over her shoulder as she bounded up the steps. "But right now we need to see PaleoJoe before he forgets we are coming, or gets lost in the Tombs, or goes home for lunch. Any of which are possible you know!"

Shelly lunged through the front doors. Dakota skidded after her and into the Balboa lobby. Today they were met by a hum of activity much busier than usual. Even Shelly had to do some fancy maneuvering to miss plowing into someone. Workmen with yellow ladders were hanging huge banners from the balcony in the main rotunda. The long banners were dark blue edged with gold and showed the picture of one of the most fearsome dinosaurs Dakota had ever seen–*Utahraptor*.

Shelly paused for a minute in the swirl of work people to admire the banners.

"This exhibit is sure going to be terrific!" she said excitedly. "It will be the biggest display of raptors ever! PaleoJoe is going to be famous for putting this together. I hope he'll let us help him. I know all about raptors. I've read the books. I can tell you anything you want to know. Go ahead ask me. Ask me a question about raptors. I bet I know the answer."

But before he could even catch up with this breathless speech, Shelly was marching away to the old staircase that led down into the Tombs.

"Come on, Dakota. Stop standing there with your mouth open," she said. "You look like a *Dunkleosteus*, only a lot smaller of course."

"My mouth isn't open," said Dakota indignantly. He was trying to remember what a *Dunkleosteus* was as he narrowly avoided collision with a man carrying a ladder.

"Really? Then how are you managing to talk?"

29

Shelly smiled wickedly and disappeared down the stairwell before Dakota could think of a reply.

Dakota followed as quickly as he could but Shelly was moving fast. He could hear her creaking and squeaking her way down the old staircase. The wooden stairs were worn in the center by thousands of feet tramping up and down over many years. Dakota and Shelly had done their part to wear down the stairs, particularly on steps seven and eight, the steps with the most squeakability. Even today Dakota could hear that Shelly had paused on the famous steps to jiggle an extra squeak or two. This allowed Dakota to catch up to her.

Playing a quick game of tag, they leaped and laughed their way to the door of the Tombs and there they were stopped by a huge surprise.

The routine of the Dinosaur Detective Club was always the same. Shelly, and now Dakota as well, would squeak down the old wooden staircase to the basement and the door of the Tombs. This door was always kept locked in order to keep out unauthorized visitors. Standing outside this secured door, Shelly and Dakota would execute the secret knock and Bob, the maintenance chief of the museum, would open the door. Bob, with his big black beard and pirate growling voice, would have the Explorer's Question ready to ask. The Explorer's Question was a difficult question about dinosaurs or fossils that had to be answered correctly in order to prove a person's worthiness to enter the Tombs.

In Shelly's words, only the bravest of explorers were ever allowed to enter.

But today things were different. Today there was no one at the door to ask difficult questions. In fact, today, the door wasn't even locked. It stood wide open.

Shelly and Dakota looked at each other and then peered down the long expanse of polished linoleum floor that ended in the distance at PaleoJoe's office.

"Bob?" Shelly called out.

There was no answer.

"I don't like this," she said.

"Neither do I," Dakota agreed. "What do you think is going on?"

"I don't know," Shelly clutched Saber's bag a little closer to her side. "Let's go see if PaleoJoe is in his office."

Usually Dakota and Shelly liked to race each other down this hallway but today they walked rapidly and their footsteps echoed eerily in a strange silence. Somehow both of them knew that the Tombs were deserted.

The door to PaleoJoe's office was an old battered oak door with a frosted glass panel. A sign posted on the door read: DO NOT DISTURB.

Shelly paid no attention to this and knocked loudly on the door.

Silence was the only response.

"Do you think he did go home for lunch?" asked

Dakota nervously.

As Shelly reached out to open the door, she suddenly froze. Beside her Dakota, too, caught his breath.

"Did you hear that?" he asked.

Shelly nodded. "It sounded like someone moving around inside." Then, impatiently, she shook her head. "So what? It's probably just PaleoJoe."

"Then why didn't he answer your knock?" whispered Dakota.

"Well, there's only way to find out," said Shelly and turned the doorknob. The door swung open.

"PaleoJoe?" Shelly called out.

Inside, except for the usual clutter of fossils, rocks, empty coffee cups and books, the room was deserted.

CHAPTER SIX

THE ART OF BARGING

"He's not here," said Dakota stating the obvious.

"I wonder why we heard someone moving around," said Shelly.

"Two possibilities," said Dakota as he stood in the doorway. Neither one of them wanted to enter the spooky silence of PaleoJoe's empty office. "The window over PaleoJoe's desk is open. Maybe we just heard the rustle of papers being blown by the wind."

"What's the second possibility?" asked Shelly.

"PaleoJoe's office is haunted," said Dakota.

"Or," said Shelly, "someone is hiding in there."

And that, they both realized was a possibility. One good place to hide in PaleoJoe's office was under his huge oak desk. Even PaleoJoe himself, Dakota had once discovered, could fit under it.

"Let's go find Gamma," suggested Shelly. "Maybe she knows what's going on."

"Right." That sounded like a good plan to Dakota.

He and Shelly left the spooky silence of the Tombs and quickly returned to the bustle of the main lobby. They made their way through the crowd of visitors and workmen, around the Wooly Mammoth with its long tusks frozen gracefully in the air, under the hanging *Pterodactyl* and toward the Museum Tour Office where they would find Gamma Brooks. Suddenly, Dakota spotted several men entering the museum from the back entrance. One of them looked very familiar.

"Hey, look," said Dakota pointing. "Isn't that Detective Franks?"

"Yes it is," said Shelly excitedly.

"I bet those are plain clothes detectives with him," said Dakota now immensely interested.

"I wonder why he's coming in the back entrance," said Shelly.

"It's almost like he doesn't want to be noticed," observed Dakota.

"Too late," said Shelly. "We've noticed! Come on. Let's see where he's going."

"Right. Follow me," said Dakota, and immediately launched into his Dexter North style. Dexter North, the famous T.V. detective, was extraordinarily good at tailing suspects. Dakota, who never missed an episode, knew all his tricks. Flipping up his shirt collar and hunching his shoulders, (because for some reason that's what Dexter North always did and it made him look very James Bondish), Dakota slunk behind other people. He ducked behind display cases. He cleverly used the tail of the *Iguanodon* on display on the atrium floor for cover as he and Shelly followed Detective Franks and his men up the wide atrium staircase, which led to the second floor exhibits.

"This seems like a lot of bother," said Shelly grumpily as she began to notice the strange looks people were giving them. "After all, it's obvious where they are going."

"You can't be too careful," Dakota muttered darkly as they topped the stairs and ducked behind the skeleton of the *Dimetrodon*.

Even though there were dinosaur skeletons displayed on the main floor of the atrium, the second floor of the Balboa was the home of the main dinosaur exhibit known as Dinosaur Hall. Dakota and Shelly peered through the ribs of *Dimetrodon* and watched Detective Franks and his men turn onto the Trilobite Balcony.

After the bright light of the lobby area, there was a big difference in the muted lighting of the second floor, the bright glow of lights over display cases, and the library hush of dim hallways. One of Shelly's favorite things to do from the second floor balcony was to peek over the railing and look down on the *T-Rex* and *Diplodocus* mounts on the main floor. But today she didn't think about it as curiosity about Detective Franks took all her attention.

Dakota, with Shelly peering over his shoulder, watched as Detective Franks made his way along the balcony corridor never once glancing at the long brilliantly lit display cases which held PaleoJoe's amazing trilobite exhibit. Even Dakota was hugely impressed by the strange, science fiction looking creatures, some with delicate spines and others rolled, armadillo-like, caught in pieces of stone. PaleoJoe had collected trilobites from all over the world. It was a fabulous collection, but Detective Franks marched straight ahead and did not even glance in the cases.

"He's heading for the Raptor Room," said Dakota.

"I wonder what is going on," Shelly whispered.

Quickly and quietly Dakota and Shelly trailed Detective Franks along the Trilobite Balcony to the doorway of the Special Exhibit room. It was here that PaleoJoe was setting up the Raptor exhibit. More blue and gold banners were displayed on either side of the closed doors. A red velvet rope attached to two gold posts blocked visitors from entering the exhibit area. A sign posted by the rope informed people that the grand opening of the exhibit would take place in about ten days, thanked them for their patience and interest, and encouraged them to come back for the great, spectacular, grand opening.

As Detective Franks paused to say something to his men, Shelly and Dakota used a handy group of boy scouts as cover and made their way over to the giant reconstruction of a *Megatherium*. The giant sloth, reared onto its hind legs and reaching up into the branches of a sturdy resin tree, stood like a guard outside the entrance to the Special Exhibits room. Just a few feet away flanking the doorway into the next room, which was the Bird Hall, was a reconstruction of a fearsome *Phorusrhacos*, a gigantic, dinosaur-like carnivorous bird. Shelly, holding her blue canvas bag containing Saber, crouched behind *Megatherium*.

Dakota, somewhat nervously, took up a position behind *Phorusrhacos,* which wasn't, of course, alive, but looked like it wanted to eat him anyway. Dakota remembered Shelly telling him that this fierce creature had eaten small horses as part of its prey. Its glass eyes seemed to stare intently at Dakota. Dakota did his best to ignore his sometimes overactive imagination and turned his attention to Detective Franks.

Detective Franks and his men were just stepping over the velvet rope barrier. As Detective Franks opened the door to the Special Exhibits room there was a momentary rush of sound. Shelly and Dakota caught a glimpse of a roomful of people bustling and crowding. Then Detective Franks and his men were through and the door was shut behind them.

"Coast is clear," said Dakota stating something

Shelly could see for herself. "Come on."

But Shelly was ahead of him, emerging from her hiding place, to stand scowling at the closed doors, her hands on her hips.

"Hey, wait for me!" Dakota gave one last nervous glance at the *Phorusrhacos* and went to stand by Shelly.

"Well, I don't know about you, but I'm going in," said Shelly.

"Hold on!" Dakota grabbed her arm. "We can't just barge in there. We need a plan."

"I have a plan," Shelly informed him.

"Really?" Dakota was skeptical. "What is it?"

"It's to barge in," said Shelly. "It's an art–barging I mean. I'm actually quite good at it. Watch."

But Dakota wasn't about to be left out of anything so he was close behind Shelly as she stepped over the velvet rope. He was ready to give her whatever assistance she needed in her plan of barging.

This close to the closed doors, Shelly could plainly hear the noise of people in the room beyond. There seemed to be a lot of shouting and arguing. Was that banging the sound of hammers? Something was going on in that room and she intended to find out what it was. Delaying no longer Shelly opened the door.

The noise of the room roared out at them as Shelly, with Dakota close on her heels, demonstrated her art of barging. Then, suddenly, a violent burst of dazzling bright light exploded in their faces.

CHAPTER SEVEN

SPECTER OF DOOM

Blinking and half blinded Dakota crashed into Shelly who tripped over something on the floor at her feet and plunged into a soft, garlic smelling person who said, "Oof!"

"Are these more of your plainclothes detectives, Franks?" A woman's voice, sharp and nasal, demanded as there came another explosive flash of light.

"Okay, Ms. Pierceson. I think the Press has had enough now. I don't want to be rude, but we have, as you can see, a mess here to clean up and so I would like to ask you to leave, please. We can continue the interview later."

Dressed in his olive pants and khaki shirt, absentmindedly stroking his short graying beard, it was

PaleoJoe taking charge. He bent down to help Shelly to her feet and put a steadying hand on the shoulder of a still blinded Dakota.

"Barging in again, Miss Shelly?" PaleoJoe asked raising one eyebrow in the trick that always made Dakota envious. But Dakota missed it because just then he couldn't see much of anything except spotted lights dancing in front of his eyes.

"I don't barge," said Shelly setting the record straight. "I knock and enter. It's an art!"

"That's called barging," said PaleoJoe.

"But PaleoJoe, how else were we supposed to know what was going on?"

"She has a point," said the garlic smelling person.

It was Detective Franks.

"Du Concombre!" said Shelly affectionately using an old nickname she had once given him. It meant "some cucumber" in French. She gave him a quick hug.

The dazzle of flashing lights continued to clear from her eyes. Shelly could see that she had tripped over a jumble of bones that lay on the floor in a confused disarray. She could also see what had caused the blinding flash of light.

In the midst of the disorder of the room stood a tall and bony woman. In one hand she wielded a large camera like it was a club. In the other she had a compact tape recorder. It had been the flash on the large camera that had done the blinding.

"Well," said the woman with her sharp voice, "I think that the real story is happening right now, Mr. Dinosaur Detective. And I am suspicious that you are trying so hard to get rid of me."

Shelly scowled at the woman. "Who are you?" she demanded.

"My, my. Such bad manners in a little girl," said the woman. She smiled. Maybe it was because her eyes, covered by rings of heavy blue makeup, looked mean. Or, maybe, it was because she wore a strange shade of purple lipstick. Whatever it was about this woman, Shelly thought her smile did not look at all friendly.

Uh-oh, thought Detective Franks and Dakota and PaleoJoe. No one called Shelly Brooks a little girl and got away with it.

"I am Ms. Pierceson." As the woman nasally pronounced her name she seemed to hiss like a snake. "I am a reporter for the City News and I am here doing an important interview with PaleoJoe about his new exhibit. An exhibit, which I might add, seems to be having its share of severe difficulties. Why is that, PaleoJoe? Is it incompetence?" And she stuck the quietly whirring tape recorder under PaleoJoe's nose to record his response.

PaleoJoe looked startled for a minute and then his eyes crossed, his face turned a little red and he let loose with a huge explosive sneeze that came with its

41

very own gentle rain of paleontologist slobber.

Brilliant, thought Dakota in complete admiration.

The look Ms. Pierceson gave PaleoJoe as she withdrew her tape recorder made Dakota remember the look in the glass eye of the *Phorusrhacos*.

"I see," she said. "May I quote you on that?"

PaleoJoe took out a red checked handkerchief and blew his nose in it. He gently ran a hand over his beard and face.

"I'm sure that PaleoJoe will be more than happy for you to quote him if you can do it intelligently," said Shelly.

Ms. Pierceson looked down her nose at Shelly as though she were looking at a particularly nasty piece of overcooked broccoli. Her bronze colored hair was smoothed into a helmet-like covering on her head. It looked like it was actually made of metal because it had, apparently, so much hairspray on it. This was a fact that did not escape Shelly.

"Perhaps *you* would like to do an interview," Ms. Pierceson said, her sharp voice icily unfriendly. "I'm sure my readers would be interested to hear the views of the children that seem to be in charge of this million dollar collection."

Shelly heard the sarcasm in Ms. Pierceson's nasally voice. She was about to reply, but Detective Franks interrupted.

"Ms. Pierceson," he said. "PaleoJoe will have a statement for the Press shortly. Now it's time for you to leave."

"Yes, and just what will he say?" demanded Ms. Pierceson, not leaving. "Will he say that the museum is haunted? Will he say that the Balboa Specter of Doom has been antagonized and that this exhibit is a danger to anyone who would come to see it? Because clearly it is." She indicated the bones at her feet. "Clearly something is going on here."

Franks gave a nod of his head to one of his men who stepped forward and politely, but firmly, took Ms. Pierceson by the elbow to escort her to the door. Four other people, apparently assistants to the metal haired

woman, moved with them, scribbling in notebooks and also snapping pictures from cameras not quite as large and aggressive as Ms. Pierceson's.

"Bye-bye Ms. *Tete en metal*," said Shelly sweetly waggling her fingers in farewell. But she had underestimated Ms. Pierceson. Ms. Pierceson knew French and this time Shelly's little trick didn't work.

"Bye-bye Miss *Haut de carotte*," Ms. Pierceson blew Shelly a kiss from her purple lips and allowed herself to be shown out.

CHAPTER EIGHT

SABOTAGE!

Shelly, stunned, was turning a slow shade of red.

"Pish," said PaleoJoe. "What an awful woman. Have to allow her to interview me though. It's all part of the publicity for this Raptor exhibit. Still, nice try, Shelly."

"What did you say?" asked Dakota. "What did she say? Why are there bones all over the floor? What's the Specter of Doom?"

"Slow down," Detective Franks laughed. "Remember Dakota, a good detective must be patient. Look. Listen."

"Yeah. I remember," said Dakota. "Looking and listening here, Chief." He whipped out his black

notebook and flipped to a page. Detective Franks, producing his own notebook, did the same.

They look like twins, thought Shelly sourly.

"Okay, Shelly," said Detective Franks. "Let's start with you."

Shelly took a quick angry breath. "I called her Ms. Metal Head because she is one, you know. Her hair looks like its been bronzed into metal and I'm sure her brains are not much better."

"What did she call you?" asked Dakota, writing in his notebook.

At first Shelly was so angry she almost couldn't speak. "She called me Miss Carrot Head! I can't believe it! She called me a little girl with bad manners and a carrot head!"

Dakota tried hard not to laugh. "At least she didn't see you try to brain yourself with your own book," he said. "That would really have been something to read in the paper. YOUNG PALEONTOLOGIST BEANS SELF WITH BOOK."

"Okay you two," PaleoJoe interrupted. "That's enough. We have some real problems here we need to focus on. Look at this mess, Franks."

"I am looking," said Detective Franks. "We came as soon as we got your call. This is number three isn't it?"

PaleoJoe looked glum and nodded his head. "Yes. It's the third incident of vandalism. First there was the *Microraptor* wall cast that mysteriously fell off the wall. Then the *Velociraptor* head was replaced with a deer skull. Fortunately, Bob found the real skull in the mop closet and it was undamaged. And now this!" He gestured at the bones scattered on the floor.

Just then they were interrupted by the approach of a large man wearing the blue uniform of the museum. It was Bob the maintenance chief. He had been in the back of the room discussing some things with one of Detective Franks' men. "PaleoJoe," he said. "Sorry to interrupt, but I'm going to need to go get a different set of tools to get this back together again." He motioned to the pile of bones on the floor.

"Go ahead," PaleoJoe nodded. "How long do you think it will take?"

"Can't say exactly," Bob frowned and scratched a blunt thumb through his large black beard. "If none of the bones are damaged it shouldn't be long. Of course, if we do find damaged bones we can get replicas made. Ninety-six percent of this skeleton is recreated anyway."

The man looks like a pirate, thought Dakota, not for the first time. Tie a couple of sticks of dynamite in his beard like Blackbeard did and Bob could be his twin brother.

"The Exhibit needs to open in ten days," said PaleoJoe.

"I'll do my best," Bob boomed in his deep voice. "This is a problem though, PaleoJoe. If we can't get this vandalism stopped I don't think you will be able to open the exhibit at all. You might have to cancel it. We wouldn't want anything to fall on an unsuspecting visitor."

Picking up an orange tool kit, Bob left to go look for the things he needed to finish his job.

"*Iguanodon* gizzards!" exclaimed PaleoJoe. "That's the problem. I think that someone doesn't want us to open this exhibit."

"The Specter of Doom?" asked Dakota eagerly.

"Yes, it could be him," PaleoJoe agreed.

"You mean he's *real!*? There's really a ghost that haunts the museum?" Dakota sort of squeaked.

PaleoJoe nodded his head. "Some people think so. He is supposed to be a fellow by the name of Barnabus Johnson. He used to be a librarian up in the old research library on the fourth floor. I think I may have run into him once or twice myself."

"Really?" Dakota's eyes were wide.

"Course it was probably just the wind," said PaleoJoe. " You know how creaky this old building can be. Anyway, I think there is something else behind all this. Someone is trying to sabotage this exhibit."

CHAPTER NINE

THE RAPTOR ROOM

"This is a very important exhibit," said PaleoJoe. He was getting a bit worked up. "We've been working hard to gather together all these displays. I mean look at what we've got here! There's nothing like it anywhere!"

He gestured with his hands inviting everyone to take a good look around. Shelly and Dakota looked curiously about them. What they saw was the newly constructed Raptor Room. This would be the Special Exhibit in the Balboa for most of the summer. PaleoJoe had managed to pull together an impressive collection of dinosaur exhibits featuring *Dromeosaurids,* the fierce and terrible predators of the dinosaur world.

"Go," said PaleoJoe. "Take a look around."

Shelly didn't need to be invited twice. The large room was dominated by a group of dinosaur recreations built on slightly raised platforms.

"Those are the Fab Four," said PaleoJoe. "At least that's what I call them. Come on, let me introduce you."

He led Shelly and Dakota to the first of the dinosaur recreations.

"Meet *Dromaeosaurus*," said PaleoJoe. "That name means 'Swift-running Lizard.' He is the first raptor ever found and he may have been the last to roam the earth. He was discovered by the famous paleontologist Barnum Brown."

"Barnum Brown discovered the first *T-Rex*," said Shelly.

"That's right," said PaleoJoe. "When he found it, Brown's *Dromaeosaurus* discovery lacked the killer claw of the raptors, however, so it took awhile for scientists to figure out that our friend here was a raptor."

"Killer claw," said Dakota. "I like the sound of that."

"You wouldn't," said PaleoJoe raising an eyebrow at him, "if a pack of *Dromaeosaurus* were after you!"

"That's probably true," admitted Dakota bending down to get a closer look at the wicked curved claw on *Dromaeosaurus's* back foot.

"Over here we have the most famous raptor," said PaleoJoe leading the group to another recreation.

This recreated dinosaur was not alone on its platform. It was locked in mortal combat with another dinosaur. "This little fellow enjoys the reputation for being the meanest raptor of them all."

"I recognize him," said Dakota. "It's *Velociraptor* isn't it?"

"That's him," said PaleoJoe nodding. "He was discovered by Roy Chapman in the Gobi Desert."

"I remember you told us about Roy Chapman on the *Stegosaurus* dig," said Shelly.

"*Velociraptor* means 'Swift Thief,'" said PaleoJoe. "This is a recreation of one of the most spectacular fossil finds ever made. In 1971, two Polish paleontologists exploring in the Gobi desert found the Fighting Dinosaurs. That stocky fellow there with the bony neck frill and the parrot-like beak is a *Protoceratops*. In the ancient desert sands of the Gobi they found *Velociraptor* locked in a battle with a *Protoceratops*. They must have been overtaken by a sandstorm which suffocated them in the middle of their battle because that is exactly the way they were found 80 million years later."

"Wow," said Dakota trying to imagine an epic battle of 80 million years ago.

"*Velociraptor* has told us much more about the connection between dinosaurs and birds," said PaleoJoe. "Most dinosaurs have rib-like scales to support their stomachs. *Velociraptor* has bony plates similar to modern birds. *Velociraptor* and his relatives

51

all have an unusual joint in their wrists, which allowed them to move their wrists from side to side. They were able to use this sideways motion to trap prey."

"He has a Killer Claw, too," said Dakota.

"The claw worked like a switchblade knife," PaleoJoe explained. "The raptors could flick it forward and downward by kicking out with their powerful legs."

PaleoJoe walked over to another platform on which a raptor, bigger than either *Velociraptor* or *Dromaeosaurus* and about the size of a wolf, was joined by three brothers in an attack on a dinosaur identified by a small plaque as a *Tenontosaurus*.

"What's going on here?" asked Shelly.

"Raptors probably hunted in packs," said PaleoJoe. "Here we have a juvenile *Tenontosaurus*. By the way, a full size adult *Tenontosaurus* is about the size of a school bus. Too big for our exhibit room. But imagine this young *Tenontosaurus* grazing in a herd at the edge of a lush forest. Even though the adult *Tenontosaurus* are alert and watching, they do not detect the keen-eyed hunters watching from the cover of the forest. Those hunters are called *Deinonychus*, each one is no bigger than a wolf, but by ambushing in a pack, they could take down the largest dinosaurs in their world.

"*Deinonychus* was discovered by Dr. John Ostrom in 1964. He found them in Montana. *Deinonychus* confirmed the existence of the group of dinosaurs that we called Raptors. Dr. Ostrom also realized that instead of being sluggish, cold-blooded creatures, these dinosaurs were very active and fast.

"For almost 20 years Scientists thought that *Deinonychus* was the biggest of the raptors, but not too long ago that view had to change when we discovered this fellow right here."

At last PaleoJoe brought them to the center of the room where the pile of bones were carefully being examined by Detective Franks and his men.

"*Utahraptor,*" said Shelly reading the plaque.

"Or what's left of him anyway," said Dakota surveying the damage.

"Why is this case over here empty?" asked Shelly. She had found a case that was located just beyond the damaged *Utahraptor.* It stood out by itself and looked as though it were placed to hold something very important.

"That," said PaleoJoe, "is the case for the heart of this exhibit. In that case, I will put on display one of the rarest raptor fossils ever found."

"What is it?" asked Shelly excitedly.

"It is the Killer Claw of a *Utahraptor,*" said PaleoJoe. "It will be difficult to get however. I don't know if I can get it in time for the grand opening and I don't know if I can convince the owner that it will be safe in the Balboa."

"Might be hard with all this vandalism going on," observed Dakota.

"Exactly," said PaleoJoe. "And Ms. Pierceson has been doing her best to be sure the public is well informed about all of it."

"This is a spectacular exhibit, though," said Detective Franks in admiration. "Even I can see that."

"Thanks," said PaleoJoe. It had been hard work to gather together all the fossils, casts, and recreations of the raptors. He was proud of the exhibit.

"And so," said Shelly, "to sum up. Get this down in your notebook, Dakota."

"Ready," said Dakota flipping open his notebook, pencil in hand.

"We seem to be faced with vandalism, a haunting, an obnoxious news reporter, a rare and valuable fossil that needs to be acquired and a great exhibit that needs to open on time. Is that about it?"

"That's about it," PaleoJoe agreed.

"Then it's nothing the Dinosaur Detective Club can't handle," said Shelly grinning.

"Shelly, you are one in a million," said PaleoJoe with a happy wink. "Let's go down to my office and Sort Out the Details." Sorting Out the Details was the method PaleoJoe used to try and organize his thinking on his cases.

But as they turned to leave the room Dakota noticed something of extreme importance.

"Shelly! Where is your bag?" he said.

Startled, Shelly realized that she was no longer carrying her blue canvas bag.

"Oh no!" she exclaimed. "I must have left it by the *Megatherium*."

Quickly, Shelly and Dakota dashed out of the Raptor Room to look. Sure enough, behind the *Megatherium* Shelly found her blue canvas bag.

It was empty.

CHAPTER TEN

A STINKY CLUE

Suddenly, the *Megatherium* growled.

"*Stegosaurus* spikes!" said PaleoJoe in astonishment. "Did you hear that? Either I'm very hungry for lunch or that giant sloth just grumbled about something."

Dakota laughed. He knew what was going on and now he knew what had happened to Saber. Getting down on his hands and knees he crawled behind the *Megatherium*.

Then, suddenly, he disappeared!

"Dakota!" Shelly yelled. "Where did you go?"

"I'm the ghost of Barnabus Johnson. *OOOooooo*," said the *Megatherium* in a spooky voice that sounded a lot like Dakota Jackson's spooky voice.

"Dakota?" Shelly got down on her hands and knees and also crawled behind the giant sloth.

"Well," said Detective Franks. "I guess our giant hairy friend is getting a lot of company today."

"Wow!" Shelly's voice was slightly muffled. The top half of her had disappeared leaving only her pink high-tops visible. "Hey, PaleoJoe! Did you know that this *Megatherium* is hollow inside?"

PaleoJoe cleared his throat. This wasn't a good idea, he knew, to allow Shelly and Dakota to climb around inside valuable museum exhibits. But, as it happened, he did know the sloth was hollow. He had always thought it would be fun to get inside it. He sometimes imagined how, if one were the size of Shelly or Dakota, one might crawl inside the *Megatherium* and scare some know-it-all self appointed tour guide or some snotty gum-chewing kid with a sudden comment on the weather or a dinosaur growl. As you could see, coming from a giant sloth, such a thing would be rather startling.

"PaleoJoe? Are you listening to me?" Shelly scrabbled her way free of the giant sloth holding something securely in her arms. Dakota tumbled out after her.

"What a great hiding place," he said. He had a cobweb in his hair and a bit of sloth seemed to have rubbed off on his face making streaks of black that made Dakota look a little like a zebra. He sneezed. "Detective Franks, if you ever needed to set up surveillance on the

57

Raptor Room, this would be the place to put it."

"Or," said Detective Franks, "We could use the surveillance cameras mounted in the room itself. Which, by the way, I will be reviewing to see if it gives us some clue to our vandal."

"Well, yes. That might work too," said Dakota.

"Look, PaleoJoe," said Shelly. "I've brought you an assistant to help you in your office." And she proudly held up Saber who, unaware of the bits of sloth fur tangled in his claws, innocently looked at PaleoJoe out of lantern yellow eyes.

PaleoJoe laughed and took the young cat from Shelly. PaleoJoe liked cats.

"He's an American Bobtail isn't he," said PaleoJoe petting the soft fur along Saber's back and sides.

"Yep. His name is Saber," said Shelly.

"Very appropriate," said PaleoJoe setting Saber on his shoulder where the small cat immediately hooked tiny claws in PaleoJoe's shirt and settled down comfortably. "American Bobtails are very smart and very friendly cats. They are also known for their sense of humor."

"So you'll take him?" asked Shelly eagerly.

"I can take him for now," said PaleoJoe. "But only until you find a proper home for him. I can't keep him. I travel around too much."

"I might be able to take him," said Dakota although he knew in his heart this was probably wishful thinking. "I have to ask my mom."

"Good enough," said PaleoJoe. "Now follow me everyone and let's get down to the Tombs so we can Sort out the Details."

With Saber on his shoulder, PaleoJoe led the way to his office. As they went, Shelly told him about thinking there had been someone hiding in his office and about how the door to the Tombs had been open. But this time when they got there the door to the Tombs was locked. PaleoJoe had to use his key to open it.

"Bob must have locked it when he came back for his tools," Shelly whispered to Dakota.

Leading the way into his office PaleoJoe pulled out several stools and chairs for people to sit on. As Saber was put on the floor he saw immediately that there were many things on this ground, which would require chasing and biting. He got to work right away on a crumpled piece of paper. A powerful swipe of his paw sent the paper skittering under PaleoJoe's large desk. Saber thoughtfully watched the paper vanish in the dark cavern under the desk and decided that this was definitely a place that needed exploring properly. He scooted after the paper disappearing like a tiger in the jungle. Everyone laughed.

"Maybe I found myself a housekeeper," said PaleoJoe.

But just then Saber reappeared, only this time he was batting and pummeling on a small bit of waxed paper. He pounced, snagging it with his tiny claws,

and flung it into the air where he caught it again. Then he swished it across the room, like a small furry hockey player after a puck, to trap it against Dakota's foot.

"Whoa! Ninja Cat!" said Dakota reaching down to pick up the piece of paper. He intended to throw it again for Saber but something about it caught his attention. "What's this?" he said. It looked like a candy wrapper. Cautiously Dakota sniffed at it. It was a faint smell but he recognized it right away.

"PaleoJoe," said Dakota with an urgent note in his voice. "I think Buzzsaw has been in your office."

CHAPTER ELEVEN

SHADOWS AND SPIES

Instantly he had everyone's attention.

"Buzzsaw?" PaleoJoe blinked.

"What makes you think that?" asked Detective Franks.

"Take a sniff of this," said Dakota and offered Detective Franks the wrapper.

Detective Franks sniffed and his eyes narrowed thoughtfully.

"I've never smelled anything like that except when I was around Buzzsaw," said Dakota.

"No. Neither have I," agreed Detective Franks.

"Well, what is it?" Shelly was impatient.

Detective Franks looked at the wrapper. "It's a wrapper for some type of throat lozenge," he said.

"I've never heard of it before. *Viking*...something. I can't read it."

"*Viking Vitamin Drops,*" said PaleoJoe. "And Dakota is right. Buzzsaw must have been here because I've never met anyone else who ate *Viking Vitamin Drops.*"

"What are they?" asked Shelly.

"Actually they aren't vitamins at all," said PaleoJoe. "They are throat drops and they are made with certain fish oils and some sort of seaweed extract, I think. Anyway, you have to special order them from Norway. Buzzsaw told me all about them once. He thought I should try them. He ate them all the time."

"Which is why he was so stinky I bet," said Shelly. "And this makes sense, PaleoJoe. If Buzzsaw is here, who else would have a better reason for vandalizing your exhibit?"

"We have to be careful we don't jump to conclusions," said Detective Franks. "Just because we found this wrapper doesn't mean that Buzzsaw is here now. He could have dropped it here when he was your graduate assistant, PaleoJoe. He must have been in your office."

"Yes, that's true," said PaleoJoe. "And it isn't like my office gets cleaned on any sort of regular basis."

"And our last reports indicated that Buzzsaw was holed up somewhere in Arizona," said Detective Franks.

But no sooner had he said this, then Dakota

let out a war whoop that made everyone jump. Even Saber.

"It *is* Buzzsaw," exclaimed Dakota. "It has to be! All the clues fit." He told Detective Franks about the grasshopper he had found, and the truck Saber had found, the smell in the cab and, most importantly of all, the Arizona license plate.

"Give me the number," said Detective Franks, now very interested in Dakota's theory. "I'll have my men trace it."

So Dakota gave Detective Franks the number he had written down. Franks left immediately to see what he could find out about it.

"Wow! Good work, Dakota," said PaleoJoe.

"Good work, Saber," said Dakota, but he was pleased to have praise from PaleoJoe.

"Yes. Saber deserves some applause, too," said PaleoJoe. "Or maybe a dish of milk. Detective Franks will get on this and I bet we'll have our vandalism problem solved."

"That just leaves the valuable fossil to get," said Shelly.

"Of course," said PaleoJoe. "Now listen you two, because I need your help on this."

Shelly pulled up the spinning stool she loved, only now she restrained from spinning on it in order to hear what PaleoJoe had to say. Dakota sat on the edge of PaleoJoe's desk, his full attention ready as well. Saber went on more office explorations because there was

an immense world of dust and paper and coffee cups and bits of floaty things that needed his attention. And PaleoJoe sat in his worn, squeaky desk chair carefully avoiding the pokey spring that sometimes got him, if he wasn't careful. He had started calling it his Crocodile Chair.

"The fossil," he said, "is extremely rare. It is a complete foot fossil of a *Utahraptor* with the 15 inch slasher claw still attached. Here is a picture of it."

"The Killer Claw," said Shelly studying the photograph PaleoJoe had handed her. "I know all about those claws."

64

Of course she does, thought Dakota in disgust. How one little girl could hold so much information in that carrot top of hers was probably one of the wonders of science.

"Raptors were bipedal," said Professor Shelly, handing the photo to Dakota. "That means they walked on two legs like we do."

"Sometimes I walk on my hands," Dakota offered. "Does that make me bihandal?" Shelly ignored him.

"On each foot," she continued, "they had those huge sickle shaped claws like the ones we just saw on the recreations in the Raptor Room. The raptors kept those claws razor sharp by holding them off the ground when they ran. Scientists think they used the claws to attack prey, sort of like cats do."

Dakota watched as Saber launched himself at another unsuspecting piece of paper and skidded, apparently out of control, under the desk. Then Dakota tried to imagine Saber as a 2000-pound killing dinosaur, the owner of the huge claw in the photograph, doing that maneuver. He felt faint as his overactive imagination successfully met the challenge.

"The owner is reluctant to allow us to display this fossil," said PaleoJoe. "He's heard about all this vandalism and he doesn't want anything to happen to his fossil. That's where you two come in."

"Great!" said Shelly. "What do we do?"

"You talk him into letting us put his fossil in the exhibit," said PaleoJoe.

65

"*Morceau de gateau!*" said Shelly spinning on the stool. "That's French for 'piece of cake', in case you didn't know."

Of course Dakota didn't know. Taking out his black notebook he flipped to the heading **Things to Do** and wrote: *Learn a language that Shelly doesn't know. Maybe Greek.*

"Who is the owner?" Dakota asked, keeping out his notebook now to record some important facts about their task. It's what any good detective would do.

"His name is Cleveland Sanders," said PaleoJoe.

Dakota wrote down the name.

"Sounds like an important man," said Shelly spinning around the other way making her ponytail swish around her head.

"Shelly, you're making me dizzy," complained Dakota.

"Good!" Shelly whirled again.

Dakota sighed. Apparently there was no way to stop the whirling dervish that was Shelly Brooks. At least not one he knew. PaleoJoe, on the other hand, did.

"He isn't a man," said PaleoJoe. "Or not exactly. He's a 12-year-old boy. He lives in Utah, and you are going to meet him tomorrow."

At this piece of information, Shelly stopped her spinning so abruptly that she fell off, leaving the stool to whir around empty.

And because Dakota was so busy laughing at her, and PaleoJoe had leaned forward to see if she was all right, no one, except Saber momentarily peeking out from under the desk, noticed the sudden shadow that appeared across the floor as the person, who had been listening outside PaleoJoe's open window moved away.

CHAPTER TWELVE

STOWAWAY

Not only were they going to Utah, but also Shelly and Dakota discovered, they were going to fly there in a private jet owned by Cleveland Sanders' dad.

"Mr. Sanders must be one rich fellow," said Shelly, as she stowed her bag and sat down on a mushroom colored couch in the center of the plane.

"What kind of name is Cleveland anyway?" she wanted to know bouncing experimentally on her seat. "Do you think he goes by Cleve? Or maybe people call him Lander. Maybe his friends call him Sandy. What do you think, Dakota?"

But Dakota didn't answer. Wearing his dark sunglasses with the unreliable lens, which could unexpectedly pop out, he seemed to be sulking. Because she was busy bouncing on the mushroom couch and thinking about Cleveland Sanders' name, Shelly didn't notice that Dakota was in his Dexter North mode. He had his shirt collar turned up and the special slouch he adopted when he was trying to imitate his hero. Keeping his black battered backpack close by his side, Dakota chose another couch across the cabin from Shelly and sat down, slouching, and looked out the window.

PaleoJoe sat in a reclining chair near another small window. He took out his book *Dinosaurs of the World* and began to read it.

The three were the only passengers. Or, at least, two of them and the pilot *thought* they were the only three passengers. Dakota happened to know differently. He knew about a fourth passenger, a stowaway.

In a short time they were airborne.

"Let's play a game," said Shelly.

"Let's not," said Dakota.

"I'll ask you a question and then you answer it," said Shelly, apparently deaf. "No, better yet, you ask the questions and I'll answer them. Make them dinosaur questions though."

"I don't know any dinosaur questions," said Dakota.

"Yes, that's probably true," said Shelly. "Oh well. Let's talk about the case then."

"What's there to talk about?" Dakota stared determinedly out of the window. Maybe, he thought, she would get bored and leave him alone.

"Dakota, what's wrong with you?" asked Shelly, studying him out of narrowed eyes. Dakota was always annoying, but there was something going on with him now that was a little out of the ordinary. Maybe it was just his sunglasses. They made him look nefarious which would have pleased Dakota, had he known about it.

"Nothing is wrong with me," said Dakota. He continued to stare out the window. "I just want to suss out the clouds."

Sussing was what Dexter North did when he needed to figure out the layout of a crime scene. Dakota thought that maybe Shelly wouldn't know that.

He was wrong. Shelly did know that. Shelly, probably, knew everything.

"You don't suss clouds," she informed him. "You suss places or suspects. Come on, Dakota, what's up?"

"Nothing," said Dakota, but just then he was betrayed.

His battered black backpack mewed.

"*Dakota!*" Shelly squealed. "Did you bring Saber with you!?"

The game was up. With a sigh Dakota unzipped his backpack, and a slightly roughed up, tailless cat scampered out.

PaleoJoe peeked over the top of his book. "Pish. Don't let him claw the upholstery," he said, and returned to reading his book.

But for the next three hours, Saber had no time to claw upholstery as he became quite busy entertaining a young paleontologist with a red ponytail and his other new friend, the boy with the black battered backpack.

Almost before they knew it, the jet was landing at the private airport in Utah where they were going to be met and driven to Mr. Sanders' home, a place called Bone Ranch.

"That's an unusual name," said Dakota when he heard it.

"We'll have to ask Mr. Sanders about it," said PaleoJoe. "Now get hold of that small tiger of yours and let's go."

Dakota stuffed Saber into his backpack and quickly followed Shelly and PaleoJoe off the plane. It was late afternoon and a hot Utah sun burned out of the sky as the three walked across the tarmac toward the small hanger. About halfway there a young man came forward to meet them. He had long black hair caught behind his neck in a ponytail. He was wearing shorts and a dark t-shirt that had the skull of a raptor on it.

"PaleoJoe? I'm Owen Patterson," he said, holding out his hand in greeting. "I work for Mr. Sanders, help him keep Bone Hill operational, you know. And I run his errands. I also collect his guests from the airport."

PaleoJoe shook hands and introduced Dakota and Shelly.

"Nice to meet you," said Owen. He had a wide, warm smile, which showed a small gap between his

71

front teeth.

"I'm afraid Dakota has abetted a stowaway on this journey," said PaleoJoe, as they began to walk toward a limousine that appeared to be waiting for them.

Owen stopped in surprise. "A stowaway? On the plane?"

"Dakota?" PaleoJoe did his eyebrow thing.

Dakota unzipped his bag just enough to allow Saber to poke his head out. Owen laughed.

"Well, we have all sorts of animals on the Ranch. I'm sure we can accommodate your stowaway just fine."

Dakota felt relieved. He hadn't really thought this through very well. After getting home the night before he had asked his mother if he could adopt Saber. His mother did not like to disappoint her son, but she knew that they could not afford to properly take care of a cat. She had had to tell him no.

Dakota had expected it, but still he felt sad. So that morning, as everyone gathered in PaleoJoe's office just before leaving, Dakota, who had been feeding and playing with Saber, had found he would not be able to leave the cat behind. He wanted the company of the little Bobtail and so, when no one was looking, he had popped Saber into his backpack and left his extra pair of jeans behind on PaleoJoe's Crocodile Chair, in order to make room.

"Come on, Dakota! Race you to the Limo!"

shouted Shelly, and took off without waiting for a response.

Dakota, always ready for a race, pelted after her, but he was hampered by his backpack. He could hear protesting yowls from Saber over this sudden, rough ride. He had to slow down.

So, for once, Shelly beat him.

She slapped triumphantly into the side of the Limo, a bit out of breath, and laughing at her success. She turned to stick out her tongue at the slower Dakota and that's when the window of the limousine whispered down and the thin, pale face of a boy peered out.

"The barbarians have arrived, I see," he sneered.

CHAPTER THIRTEEN

THE OUTLAW TRAIL

Shelly felt her face get hot with embarrassment.

"Hi," she said. "I'm Shelly Brooks and this is Dakota Jackson."

Dakota, a bit out of breath, was busy checking on Saber and so only nodded in the direction of the boy.

"I don't care," said the boy. His narrow face was pale and his gray eyes were hostile and unfriendly. Shelly was pretty certain that this must be Cleveland Sanders, and if it was, it was indeed going to be very hard to get him to allow PaleoJoe to display his valuable fossil.

The boy looked coolly at Shelly as though he were examining a bit of rumpled newspaper tossed by the wind. "You are getting grubby fingerprints on the car and Owen has just washed it."

"Are you rude naturally or do you have to practice it?" asked Shelly her temper rising.

"Pish, Shelly," said PaleoJoe appearing beside her. He eyed the boy sitting in the car. *So this is the fine fellow all the fuss is over*, he thought to himself. Shelly, he was pretty sure, would figure out a way to handle him.

"Cleveland, I don't suppose I could get you to get out of the car and help our guests with their bags, could I?" asked Owen approaching.

Without a word the window shimmered up and the car door remained closed.

"No, of course not," said Owen, in exasperation.

Owen opened the trunk of the car and PaleoJoe and Shelly dumped in their bags. Dakota kept his backpack with him of course, as it contained a passenger.

Owen opened the door of the limousine for Shelly and smiled at her as she paused a minute to peer into the sumptuous interior.

"Wow," she said.

"A ride for a princess," said Owen, with a wide smile.

Shelly scowled. "I'm a scientist," she informed him.

"My mistake," Owen apologized. "This is a ride for a V.I.P. then."

"Very Important Paleontologist," said Shelly smugly and got in.

PaleoJoe and Dakota followed her. Dakota's backpack had started to growl again.

Cleveland Sanders waited until they had all piled inside and then, without a word, he got out of the car and went to sit in the front with Owen.

"Well," said PaleoJoe to Shelly. "It looks like you and Dakota will have your work cut out for you."

"Not the friendliest fish in the sea," said Dakota, unzipping his bag to let Saber out.

"He's a true *Dunkleosteus* for sure," Shelly sighed. She slumped in her seat and began to imagine various unpleasant situations for Cleveland Sanders to deal with. These ranged from getting trapped in very sticky tar to being chased by mad *Utahraptors*.

Meanwhile Dakota and Saber explored the limousine. Saber marched along the backs of the seats and decided that, of all places, he liked the spot recently vacated by Cleveland Sanders. There he went into his bread loaf pose, tucking his toes under his chest, and watched with unblinking yellow eyes the shadowy tops of the rocky landscape sliding by out the window.

Dakota tried the various buttons and learned that not only could he make all the windows slide up and down, but a square in the roof slid back as well. He found the small phone that connected him to Owen and was informed by Owen himself that it would take 45 minutes to get to the Ranch, and if anyone was thirsty there was some pop in the refrigerator. They could help themselves.

"Wow," said Dakota opening the small refrigerator and peering inside. "It's like having your own grocery store!"

Discovering the refrigerator held Orange Cream Soda, he helped himself. "Now all I need is some beef jerky," he said. Hopefully, he telephoned Owen in the front of the car and asked him. There wasn't any beef jerky, but when Owen stopped at a convenience store and went in and bought him some, Dakota felt very happy indeed.

"Tell us what you know about Cleveland Sanders and his dad," Shelly requested of PaleoJoe as she sipped her own bottle of Orange Cream Soda.

"Well," PaleoJoe smoothed a hand over his beard, "I know Cleveland's dad fairly well, but I don't know Cleveland at all. Richard Sanders, that's Cleveland's dad, is a very wealthy businessman. He has donated exhibits to the Balboa before. He's very interested in paleontology."

"Is that why his ranch is called Bone Ranch?" asked Dakota.

"I don't know for sure," said PaleoJoe. "It's an interesting place. It was part of the Outlaw Trail."

"Oh, man!" Dakota exclaimed, almost spilling his Orange Cream Soda as he suddenly sat forward on hearing this fact. He couldn't believe it. "The Outlaw Trail? Are you kidding me!? Butch Cassidy and the

Hole in the Wall Gang and everything?" He bobbed up and down a little in his extreme excitement and instantly forgot about his Orange Cream Soda, the beef jerky, and the cool buttons, and even the purring Saber because, if Time Machines were real, Dakota knew that after going back to the Civil War to meet Allan Pinkerton of the famous Pinkerton Detectives, the next place he would go would be to the Outlaw Trail to meet Butch Cassidy.

"Tell me everything," he said.

Just then the limousine left the smoothness of the paved highway for the bumpy roll of a dirt road. The back seat phone rang.

Dakota answered it. "Hello?"

He expected it to be Owen, but it wasn't. "Welcome to the Outlaw Trail, Butch," Cleveland Sanders' voice was a snotty sneer and then he hung up.

"Okay," said Dakota, hanging up the phone. "I don't know how he is doing it, but somehow that polite boy, Cleveland Sanders, is listening to everything we are saying."

"Is that a fact?" There was a dangerous light in Shelly's eye.

Yep, thought Dakota to himself, *I bet that is exactly how the outlaws looked just before they dynamited open a bank vault.*

CHAPTER FOURTEEN

BONE RANCH

"I think we should give that most polite and courteous boy something to listen to, don't you?" said Shelly, with a wicked, outlaw grin on her face. "PaleoJoe, a little *Baby Elephant's Walk,* if you please?"

"Pish," said PaleoJoe, but he was grinning too and so, lightly tapping on his knee, he began to hum the tune that Shelly had requested.

"Now, ladies and gentlemen, for your listening pleasure," said Shelly pretending she was announcing a song on the radio, "here is a little song that I just made up."

And she began to sing along with PaleoJoe's humming. Dakota punctuated Shelly's song with

dramatic popping noises he made by flicking a finger out of the side of his mouth. It was one of his many talents. Saber decided he needed to take a bath, and so maybe he wasn't listening at all.

"Once I went exploring in the country," sang Shelly.

"For bones..." (pop, pop)

"Dinosaur bones..." (pop, pop)

"Take it Dakota!"

"I found something extraordinary..." Dakota improvised singing loudly.

"It was bones..." (pop, pop)

"Dinosaur bones..." (pop, pop)

"Over to you PaleoJoe," shouted Dakota, and he and Shelly took up the hum while PaleoJoe made up the final verse.

"The biggest find of the Century," PaleoJoe sang, largely off key.

"T-Rex and Stegosaurus!" (pop, pop, pop)

"All bones..." (pop, pop)

"Fossilized bones..." (pop, pop, pop)

And the three broke into loud laughter because PaleoJoe's verse hadn't exactly fit the music.

The limousine came to a smooth stop.

"Uh-oh," whispered Dakota. "Maybe they didn't like our singing and we're going to have to walk the rest of the way."

But when the door opened, a smiling Owen said, "Welcome to Bone Ranch."

The air was chilly as Shelly got out of the limousine. The sun had sunk behind the mountains and everything was in a cool blue twilight. The moon was clearly visible as a thin crescent low on the horizon. Shelly could see that they had come to a stop in the driveway in the middle of a large sprawl of buildings. Through a nearby stand of cottonwoods she could hear the splash of a fast moving river. Cleveland was already walking away from them, heading toward a big ranch house wrapped by a large porch and glowing with friendly light.

"Thanks, Owen," said PaleoJoe shaking hands. "That was a smooth ride."

"No problem," said Owen. "You will be staying with me in the bunk house. It's that long dark building just beyond the trees. I'll take your bags over. Oh, and I enjoyed the concert," he said, and hefting PaleoJoe's bags to his shoulder Owen swaggered away into the twilight happily humming *Baby Elephant's Walk*.

"Come on, Dakota," said Shelly impatiently.

"I'm coming," said Dakota. He had needed to snug Saber in his backpack but, after a comfortable limousine ride, Saber had other ideas. Dakota, being bigger and stronger, had won in the end and, backpack secured, he tumbled out of the car.

But as he stepped out of the limousine, Dakota was frozen in his tracks as suddenly, out of the calm twilight, came a long eerie cry. It sounded like a baby wailing or maybe it was the moaning of some injured

animal. It was followed by a series of short yips that stabbed into the quiet of the night.

The hair on the backs of Dakota's arms stood up on end. "Shelly?" he asked nervously. "Do you think the ghost of Barnabus Johnson followed us here?"

CHAPTER FIFTEEN

THE ANSWER IS NO

Shelly saw Cleveland Sanders in the light of the porch turn around. He was laughing at them. Shaking his head, the boy disappeared inside the house.

"Relax, Dakota," said Shelly catching her breath. "I think it's only coyotes."

"Coyotes!" Dakota clutched his backpack close. He could feel Saber wiggling fearfully around inside.

As the eerie howls and yips came again, Dakota noticed that Shelly had whipped out her space age cell phone and was making a recording of the unearthly sounds.

"I've never heard anything like that before in my whole entire life," said Dakota nervously. "Do coyotes eat people?"

"I don't think so," said Shelly, and played back her recording.   It sounded pretty real. Too real for Dakota.

"PaleoJoe! It's good to see you again!" This greeting came from a large man standing on the porch of the big house and waving. "Come on in. You must all be tired and hungry."

"That's Mr. Sanders," said PaleoJoe waving back a greeting. "Come on you two, let's go and meet him."

"I certainly hope he has better manners than his son," said Shelly, under her breath.

"I just hope the coyotes don't attack," said Dakota, hurrying after her.

"Don't worry about it," said Shelly over her shoulder. "I'll lay a few Kung Fu moves on them. They won't mess with me."

And Dakota felt that she was probably right.

Richard Sanders turned out to be nothing like his son. He was a kind and generous man. Large and a bit loud, he gave the appearance of a person who enjoyed comfort and a lot of food. His ranch house, too, was big and open, full of comfortable looking sofas and big reading chairs each with its own floor lamp. Mr. Sanders welcomed them all, including Saber, and immediately whisked everyone into a grand tour of his home.

"Of course, the ranch house is new. Built it myself when Cleveland was born. But the other buildings, you probably saw a bit of them when you drove in, were built by my great grandpa, Barfield Sanders. It was diamonds, you know," he said tapping Dakota on the shoulder. Dakota nodded as though he understood, but he was actually not that interested.

"There was supposed to be this diamond mine here, but it proved to be a hoax. My great grandpa didn't figure it out in time and he had bought up all this land here. See?"

They had come to a large framed map on the wall. Mr. Sanders traced the territory of his land with a well-manicured finger.

"Old Barfield wasn't all stupid though. He chose this location here because there is a naturally occurring river crossing."

"I thought I could hear water," said Shelly.

"Of course," said Mr. Sanders. "I could tell just by looking at you that you were a sharp thinker."

Shelly enjoyed this compliment.

"This spot was used by Indians, fur trappers, travelers and outlaws."

"Like Butch Cassidy?" asked Dakota eagerly.

"Exactly like Butch Cassidy," said Mr. Sanders with a wink. "Now follow me. We'll settle down in this room just over here."

Mr. Sanders led them into a big room. A gentle evening breeze from several open windows billowed

the dark plaid curtains that hung to the floor. The walls were lined with bookshelves and there were some display cases of fossils that Shelly tried to get a closer look at as Mr. Sanders whirled them along. Finally, much to PaleoJoe's satisfaction, a big fireplace with a cheerful blaze of fire warmed the room. Here there was a table of sandwiches and hot soup waiting for them and as much root beer as Dakota could hold—which turned out to be a fair amount.

"Why do you call your ranch Bone Ranch?" asked Shelly as soon as she could get a word in.

"Well, because, my young paleontologist," said Mr. Sanders, "what else would you call a place that had its very own bone mine?"

Shelly's eyes grew wide. "What kind of bones?"

"There isn't anything like it that I've ever seen," Mr. Sanders continued. "Cleveland here has explored it as much as anyone. He can tell you about it."

Cleveland Sanders had just entered the room, but it was clearly because he had been requested to and not because he wanted to. He frowned at his dad and went over to the table of food to make himself a sandwich.

"But there will be plenty of time to see all that," Mr. Sanders boomed on. Shelly frowned, her curiosity unsatisfied. "Tomorrow Cleveland is going to take you folks over to Dinosaur National Monument, a place I know PaleoJoe likes a little bit."

PaleoJoe, of course, was grinning like a kid in

a candy store, which suggested that he liked the place a bit more than a little. "I do like the DNM," he said rubbing his hands together. "Fascinating place. In fact I have a friend who used to work there. I wonder if Mike..."

"I thought Owen was going to take them," interrupted Cleveland. Shelly thought he sounded annoyed and was secretly glad. His company was the least desirable but somehow she and Dakota were going to have to convince this kid to let PaleoJoe display the valuable raptor fossil he owned. Mr. Sanders was obviously trying to get them that opportunity.

"Owen will drive. You will guide. Take the jeep."

Cleveland apparently knew when he couldn't argue with his dad. "Fine," he said. "I'll take you, but don't expect me to loan you my fossil, PaleoJoe. The answer is no! Your museum isn't good enough for it."

Angrily he thumped his plate hard on the table and marched from the room leaving his half eaten sandwich behind.

CHAPTER SIXTEEN

BUTCH

Shelly rose early the next morning and, taking Saber with her, went outside to look around. It was like walking back into time. Shelly found herself surrounded by old buildings built over a hundred years ago by Barfield Sanders himself. The wood was weathered and splintery, but the buildings looked like they were being kept in good condition. And it was quiet.

Eerily quiet.

Saber stayed close to Shelly as the two of them began to explore.

"Stick close and watch out for snakes," Shelly warned him.

"*Mmerrow*," said Saber which in some languages

meant, 'You bet I will!'

"That's a pretty smart cat you have." The voice came out of the shadows of a nearby building and made Shelly jump.

"He's an American Bobtail," said Shelly as a shadowy figure emerged from the gloom of the old building. "They are a smart breed of cat."

It was Cleveland Sanders. He was dressed in jeans, a cowboy hat and a light colored short-sleeved shirt. To Shelly he seemed more relaxed and not so hostile. He wasn't being exactly friendly but he also wasn't insulting her either.

"I could tell that by that furry stump on his backside," said Cleveland. He waggled his fingers in the stalks of grass. Saber, always willing to play a quick game of Brave Hunter, crouched and attacked. Cleveland laughed. "He looks like a small bobcat."

What a strange person, thought Shelly. He had a nice laugh for such a sour boy and when he smiled his face didn't look mean at all.

"What is this place?" she asked thinking that this might be her one chance to get to know this difficult boy.

"This particular building was the General Store in Barfield Sanders' time," Cleveland pulled grass growing near the edge of the building and began to chew on it.

"So this was a town?" asked Shelly. She was keeping one eye on Saber who seemed to be interested

in maybe exploring under the dark porch overhang.

Cleveland made a little whistle noise and distracted the cat back toward them by brushing the piece of grass invitingly. Saber, feeling very happy, launched an attack. Cleveland laughed again, but somehow Shelly felt that his good mood could disappear just as easily as it had appeared.

"This wasn't a town, exactly," Cleveland continued to play with Saber but, a little surprisingly, answered Shelly's question. "It was a sort of business that Barfield Sanders ran. He had this store and over there is the blacksmith shop. The corral is a little broken down as you can see but it was made with hand-hewn railroad ties which drifted down the river over there. Those things are practically indestructible. A lot of travelers came through here to cross the river. Barfield saw an opportunity to make some money."

"What is that smaller building back there?" Shelly pointed to a small stone house nestled closer to the river.

"Come on," said Cleveland. "I'll show you."

Dragging his feet invitingly for Saber to pounce on, Cleveland led the way through tall scrub grasses to the building shaded by an ancient cottonwood tree. They were quite close to the river here and Cleveland scooped up Saber to set him on his shoulders. "I know cats can swim," he said. "But the current is swift here and we don't want to take any chances."

Shelly watched the deep green water swirl by. It

wasn't a huge river but she could see how a crossing point would be necessary especially if the river was as deep as it seemed to be.

"This is the Stone House," said Cleveland. "It was mostly used for cool storage. It was built by an outlaw named Morris Patterson."

"Was he any relation to Owen?" asked Shelly.

"Maybe," said Cleveland. "Owen doesn't know exactly. He's over here. I'll introduce you."

"Who is over here?" asked Shelly. "Owen? We already met remember?"

"Not Owen. Morris," said Cleveland, and pushed aside some tall grasses so Shelly could see that they were actually standing in a small cemetery. An ancient gravestone leaning to one side bore a faint inscription. Shelly could just make out the words *Morris Patterson* and a date, 1867.

"Wow," said Shelly. "We have to show this to Dakota."

"Hey, Shelly!!" It was Dakota himself hailing them.

"Over here, Dakota," Shelly called. "You have to see this!"

Dakota jogged over and stood looking down at the gravestones completely and totally amazed. Shelly and Cleveland stared at Dakota completely and totally amazed as well.

"Dakota," said Shelly exchanging a bewildered look with Cleveland. "What did you do to your hair? I only ask because you appear to be–um–bald."

Dakota laughed. "I'm not bald. There's still some there. Look, you can feel it!" And he bent his head down so Shelly could see that there was indeed a small amount of peach fuzz hair still covering his head. She cautiously reached out to feel and discovered that Dakota's head felt like it was covered in a soft, nappy cloth like velvet.

"Dakota, what did you do?"

"Do you like it? It's a Butch cut," Dakota said grinning. "You know, the kind you get in the army? Owen helped me."

Shelly only had one response, "Why?"

"So you can call me Butch, of course," said Dakota nodding and grinning and, getting carried away, slapped Cleveland on the back.

Cleveland plucked Saber from his shoulder and dropped him onto the ground. "I'm baby sitting freaks," he said. He turned his back on Shelly and Dakota and walked away.

CHAPTER SEVENTEEN

DINOSAUR NATIONAL MONUMENT

"Come on, Butch," said Shelly to Dakota. "Do you know that your head looks smaller without your hair?"

"Feels lighter, too," said Butch, a.k.a. Dakota Jackson.

"That's because your brains fell out and rolled away," said Shelly.

"Very funny," said Dakota running the palm of his hand over his new haircut. Anyway, he liked it.

Shelly and Dakota took Saber back to the ranch and gave him into the care of Mr. Sanders who said he would look after the small cat while the others went for their visit to Dinosaur National Monument. PaleoJoe took one look at Dakota's new haircut, raised one of his eyebrows and said, "Pish."

"I'll get the jeep," said Owen. He was dressed, as usual, in shorts, but today his t-shirt displayed a *T-Rex* in full roar. When he brought the jeep around, they all piled in. PaleoJoe sat in the back with Dakota and Shelly, one on each side of him. Cleveland had gotten into the front seat without asking anyone anything. Shelly noticed that the closed, angry look was back on his face.

They jounced and bounced around as Owen took the dirt road out to the paved highway but, once they hit that, it was smooth riding. The wind blew through the open jeep, hot and dusty in their faces. Cleveland said nothing, just stared out at the rocky landscape. Owen concentrated on driving and PaleoJoe did all of the talking. Even though he was sitting right next to Shelly and Dakota he still had to yell to make himself heard.

"You're going to see the largest quarry of Jurassic period dinosaur bones ever discovered," he shouted. The wind whipped his hat, threatening to pull it off his head. PaleoJoe planted one hand on top of it to keep it in place. "It was discovered in 1909 by a paleontologist named Earl Douglass. He was from Iowa, but he worked for the Carnegie Museum of Pittsburgh, Pennsylvania. President Woodrow Wilson made it a

National Monument in 1915. If my friend Mike is still working there we should get V.I.P. treatment!"

Soon Owen was pulling into a parking lot outside of a strange looking three-sided building of jutting angles and windows. It seemed to grow right out of a cliff that formed the 4th wall of the structure.

"I'll wait here for you," said Cleveland, pulling out a paperback book and settling himself in the seat of the jeep. "I've seen it all before."

"Suit yourself," said Owen.

Shelly and Dakota piled out of the jeep and took a look around. Right away Dakota spotted a replica of a stegosaurus placed on a gravel bed just outside of the strange building. Shelly looked out across a landscape of rocks and sky. There seemed to be a lot of sky. It made her feel small.

"Inside that building," said PaleoJoe, "is a rock wall containing 1,500 fossil bones. That rock layer forms one whole wall of this structure. Paleontologists have carefully chipped away the rock to leave the bone exposed so people can study them in the natural setting of a dig. There is nowhere like it anywhere on the planet. Follow me!"

Eagerly PaleoJoe pushed forward. Shelly, Dakota and Owen followed.

Inside was a sight that made Shelly catch her breath in amazement. Following PaleoJoe they made their way onto a balcony that overlooked the famous cliff wall of dinosaur bones. The bones could be seen

clearly as they jutted out from the gray cliff face. People dressed in white coveralls and protective goggles were working on the bones. Some people were suspended from scaffolding, others were sitting in the rock face itself. They were using small tools, brushes and picks but some were using large pneumatic hammers.

"I don't see Mike working on the cliff," said PaleoJoe. "Stay here. I'm going to ask somebody."

"Wow," said Shelly. She barely heard him.

"*Stegosaurus* Teeth," said Dakota, feeling a dinosaur reference to be appropriate here.

"It really is something to see, isn't it?" said Owen.

"How did all those bones get there like that?" asked Shelly.

"That wall," said Owen, "is part of a special kind of rock layer of sand and gravel that has alluvial origins. Do you know what that means?"

"Alluvial," repeated Shelly thinking hard. "I think PaleoJoe told me that means from a river bed."

"That's right," said Owen. "The alluvial rock layer in this area is called the Morrison Formation. It is from the Late Jurassic Period and has proven to be the richest source of dinosaur fossils in North America."

"Look at the way those bones are jumbled together," Dakota observed. "It looks like they were just piled up in one spot."

"Well, in a way you are right about that," said Owen. "This place that is now the Quarry, was once a channel of a river. It was a river that collected and buried these thousands of dinosaur bones."

"What kinds of dinosaurs are found here?" asked Shelly.

"What is the largest creature to ever walk on land?" asked Owen.

Shelly smiled. He sounded like Bob back at the Balboa asking an Explorer's Question. *"Sauropods,"* she answered.

"Right," said Owen nodding. "They were huge, long-necked, long-tailed, plant-eating dinosaurs and they were the dominant animals of the late Jurassic Period. The bones of *Sauropods* make up about three-fourths of all the fossils found here."

"I sure would like to get on that cliff face and do some digging," said Shelly.

"Sorry to disappoint you," said PaleoJoe returning to the group just as Shelly made this wish. "But my friend Mike doesn't work here anymore. I'm afraid that for today it will just have to be looking."

Shelly felt a little disappointed by this but still, there was a lot to see. She and PaleoJoe wandered down to the second level. Owen went off to shop for t-shirts in the gift store and Dakota decided to go back outside to check out the *Stegosaurus* statue. He thought that maybe he would try to sketch it.

The sun was hot and bright as he emerged from the cool interior of the building. Fumbling in his pocket, Dakota found his sunglasses and put them on.

There was the *Stegosaurus,* but his sketchbook was in the jeep. Dakota started down the wide steps leading around the side of the building when something caught his eye. He made a dive for the nearest cover–a brown garbage can sticky and home to about four thousand flies.

But Dakota didn't even notice. He peered around the edge of the garbage can. From this vantage point he could clearly see the jeep. There was Cleveland Sanders sitting in the jeep. And there was the tall, skinny figure of a man bent over the door of the jeep having a conversation with Cleveland. A figure Dakota didn't have any trouble recognizing.

It was Buzzsaw.

CHAPTER EIGHTEEN

DEAD MAN'S ROAD

"IsawBuzzsawintheparkinglotwithCleveland," gasped Dakota.

Shelly frowned at him. "Are you trying to say something about bees?" she asked him.

Shelly and PaleoJoe were now on the lower level of the Visitor Center. They were still finding interesting things to look at on the cliff wall. Dakota had run all over looking for them and he was seriously out of breath.

"Slow down, Dakota," said PaleoJoe. "You do sound like you have a mouthful of bees with all this buzzing and sputtering."

"And you spit on me," said Shelly.

Dakota took a deep breath and tried again. "I saw Buzzsaw in the parking lot talking to Cleveland."

"Are you sure?" asked Shelly. "How would he know where to find us?"

"Of course I'm sure. And I didn't spit on you," Dakota assured her. "He could have found us easily. I bet PaleoJoe had his office window open when we were discussing this trip."

"Yes. I think I did have that window open," said PaleoJoe thinking back.

"Well," said Dakota connecting the dots for Shelly who looked confused. "We know that Buzzsaw was lurking around. He probably stood outside the window and heard everything we said." Dakota knew this was very possible, having done something similar himself once.

"This could be serious," said PaleoJoe. "Follow me. Keep your eyes open." He quickly led the way back outside. Dakota and Shelly were close behind him.

"But we didn't know we were going to visit Dinosaur National Monument then," said Shelly.

"Where else would PaleoJoe go?" asked Dakota.

"He's right," said PaleoJoe. "There's the jeep. I see Cleveland and that's Owen sitting beside him, but I don't see anyone else."

"Are you sure it wasn't Owen you saw?" asked Shelly.

"Positive," said Dakota. "Buzzsaw is tall and thin. He was leaning on the door talking to Cleveland. Owen is shorter. He's wearing a hat and he has that ponytail. It wasn't him."

"I'll handle this," Dakota added. And before anyone could stop him he was at the jeep and had launched into Dexter North mode.

"Okay, Cleveland," said Dakota. "I saw you with my own eyes and so you may as well tell us all about it."

"Look, Butch," said Cleveland. "I don't know what you are yammering about and, shocking as it might seem to you, I don't care."

"Sorry, Cleveland," Shelly tried to apologize. How was it going to help getting this boy mad at them? She wanted to thump Dakota on the head. "It's just that Dakota saw you talking to somebody we know."

"So what?" demanded Cleveland.

"Exactly," said PaleoJoe stepping in and interrupting Dakota's interrogation. "Now get in the jeep, both of you. It's time we left here."

I bet Dexter North didn't have people interrupting his interrogations, thought Dakota grumpily as he climbed in after Shelly.

Owen put the jeep in gear and pulled out of the parking space. "If you aren't in a hurry to get home," he said, "I thought I would just show you something very cool while we are here in the Monument."

"That would be great," said PaleoJoe. But as Owen drove away from the Visitor Center, Dakota noticed that PaleoJoe kept turning around to look behind them.

"Are you thinking we might be followed, PaleoJoe?" asked Dakota quietly.

"It's a possibility," said PaleoJoe. "Look what I found on the ground by the jeep." He held up a *Viking Vitamin* wrapper.

Dakota's eyes got wide. "He was here, then!"

"Looks like it," said PaleoJoe.

Meanwhile, Owen had been driving them up a steep and narrow road pitted with potholes, which jostled everyone around somewhat.

"Cleveland thought you would like to see this," said Owen over his shoulder.

"See what? A million potholes?" asked Dakota as he jounced against PaleoJoe.

"Not many people come up this way because the road is so bad," admitted Owen.

"It's called Dead Man's Road," said Cleveland swiveling around to give Dakota a sinister stare. Or at least Dakota felt that it was a sinister stare.

Trying hard not to get whiplash, Shelly held tightly to the door strap and closed her eyes. It was a little like riding a bucking bronco, she thought. Not that she had actually ever ridden a bucking bronco, but she imagined it would feel just like this, with your head flapping around as though it would fly right off your neck, and go rolling back down the cliff.

Then, suddenly, they stopped and Shelly, finding her head still attached to her neck, opened her eyes. What she saw made her gasp with astonishment.

CHAPTER NINETEEN

A RAPTOR ENCOUNTER

They had come to a stop on top of a high level lookout. Some wind-twisted pines gave a scraggy sort of shade where Owen parked the jeep. Stretched at their feet was a great expanse of canyons and plateaus where the rock formations showed colored layers as though thin slabs of stone had been piled one on top of the other.

They all got out of the jeep to look.

"Wow," said PaleoJoe.

"I thought you might enjoy it," said Cleveland. "It's a pretty good look at the Morrison Formation."

Cleveland puzzled Shelly. One minute he was a complete and total snot. The next minute he was a thoughtful guide. It was almost as though he had to work at being nasty, she thought. It seemed complicated.

"That sure is a lot of wilderness," said PaleoJoe.

"If you hike up that trail over there," Cleveland pointed, "you can get an even better view."

"Come on, then! What are we standing around here for?" said PaleoJoe eagerly and set off at a brisk walk.

"You go ahead and go with him," said Dakota to Shelly. "I want to stay here and keep on eye on things."

Shelly nodded and scampered after PaleoJoe. Cleveland gave Dakota a grin. "Too much exertion for you, Butch?" he said and pulled out his book. He settled himself in the sparse shade of the old pines and began to read.

"Too much exertion for me," said Owen. "Think I'll catch a little cat nap." Stretching out in the jeep with his feet dangling over the passenger side door, Owen laid his hat over his face. It wasn't long before Dakota could hear him snoring.

Shelly scrambled in the scrub after PaleoJoe.

"This sure is a steep climb," she said.

PaleoJoe, puffing a little bit and sweating a lot, agreed with her. "I think we are almost there," he said.

A few minutes more brought them to the top of the trail and the view was spectacular. The cliffs and canyons spread out below them in shadowed hollows and sun baked tops. There seemed to be a haze on the horizon that gave a tint of blue to everything. And overhead was the ocean of sky.

"Big sky," said Shelly. She had never seen so much sky. There were no clouds in that expanse of the bluest color of blue and it seemed to go on forever.

"It's beautiful," said PaleoJoe.

A giant boulder offered a place to sit and both PaleoJoe and Shelly took advantage of it. There was no shade here. The dead twisted branches of a nearby tree seemed to prove how difficult it would be to live in this high world.

Shelly and PaleoJoe sat in silence listening to a hum of hidden insects and gazing out across the vista of canyon and sky. And then Shelly saw something on the very far horizon. High up. At first it was just a dark freckle against the bright blue but gradually it grew bigger.

"What's that?" asked Shelly.

PaleoJoe squinted against the bright sun. "I think it is a bird," he said. And then after watching it for a few seconds more he added, "A big bird."

It came closer. Eventually Shelly could see that it was, indeed, a big bird gliding, with an impressive wingspan on the invisible currents of air, high in the blue world of the sky. The bird was making lazy circles, wings outspread, drifting closer.

"It's riding on the heat currents," said PaleoJoe.

"What kind of bird is it?" asked Shelly.

105

"I'm not sure," said PaleoJoe. "But I think it's an eagle. Let's watch. It's coming our way."

Shelly and PaleoJoe sat very still and watched the great bird gliding in the sky. It came closer and closer until PaleoJoe could tell by the rounded wings of its profile that it was, indeed, an eagle.

"It's one of the great and rare Golden Eagles," said PaleoJoe excitedly.

It was so close now that Shelly could actually see the feathers, like long, sensitive fingers, spread at the tips of its wings.

And then, the eagle did a very splendid thing. As though the bird was as curious about the two humans sitting in this high place as the humans were of him, the eagle folded his wings and landed in the branches of the dead tree just a few feet away from where Shelly and PaleoJoe sat on their rock.

Shelly made herself very still so not to scare it away. Beside her PaleoJoe had also turned into a statue. The bird turned his head, covered with beautiful golden brown feathers that seemed to reflect the light of the sun, and regarded them out of one bright, dark colored eye. The eagle's legs were covered with feathers and looked, Shelly thought, just like he was wearing feathery trousers. The eagle gripped the dead branch with powerful looking talons. His curved beak was long and looked very capable of tearing into prey.

After several minutes of silent regard, the eagle unfolded his wings, which stretched to a length that was longer than Shelly was tall. As though standing on tiptoe, the eagle launched himself off the dead branch with enough force that Shelly and PaleoJoe could hear it creak, then, beating his wings hard, the eagle climbed back into the sky. Once there, he dipped and tumbled as though happy to be airborne again.

"Look!" said Shelly. "He's sky dancing!"

And then, at last, the eagle flattened out his wings and circled on the hot air away from Shelly and PaleoJoe and toward the far distant desert horizon.

CHAPTER TWENTY

OUT OF CONTROL ON DEAD MAN'S ROAD

"Did you see that? PaleoJoe, did you *see that!!?*" Shelly jumped up and down and pointed in the direction of the disappearing eagle.

"Yes," said PaleoJoe a broad grin spreading over his face. "I was sitting right here. I saw it too."

"He was *huge!*" shouted Shelly. "He must have been as big as a tank! He was gigantic!"

"Don't exaggerate," said PaleoJoe squinting to watch the tiny, far away dot that was the eagle.

"Well he was much bigger than me anyway," said Shelly. "And he was almost bigger than you! Come on! Let's go tell everybody what we saw. It was an eagle! A real eagle! He looked right at me! He was huge! Come on, PaleoJoe!"

Shelly, already in full gallop down the trail, quickly disappeared. With a shake of his head and smiling to himself over the wonders of nature and small tornado-like girls with red hair, PaleoJoe followed.

When he reached the scraggly pines and the jeep, PaleoJoe was feeling very hot and very thirsty, so he was greatly surprised, and enormously pleased, to discover that Owen had spread out a picnic. A bright red cloth covered the ground. A huge cooler that had been stowed unnoticed in the back of the jeep had been opened. Sitting around the cloth, the others were already busy slurping down sodas and munching on chips and sandwiches. PaleoJoe happily joined them.

Shelly was still in her nonstop exclaiming over the eagle, only now half her story became gurgles and lip smackings as she tried to drink her soda and tell her story at the same time.

"He was all golden brown on his...*gurgle*...neck and he had feathers on his legs...*gurgle, smack*...just like he was wearing pants and..." And at last she gave herself the hiccups. "He...*hic*...was right there on a... *hic*...branch and I could almost...*hic*...touch him."

"Hi, PaleoJoe," Owen greeted him. "We've been hearing about your adventure."

PaleoJoe nodded. "It was really amazing," he said.

109

"Well, here," Owen handed him a cup of something that was ice cold and PaleoJoe was as happy as he had ever been when he discovered that it contained iced coffee. "Tell us about it."

PaleoJoe took a long sip of the refreshing iced coffee. He looked over at Cleveland who had been listening, obviously interested, to Shelly's explosive hicuppy story and realized that there was more to this kid than they knew. Maybe here would an opportunity, thought PaleoJoe.

"It was a Golden Eagle," said PaleoJoe accepting a paper plate from Owen. He began to construct himself a sandwich from the variety of meat and cheeses spread out on the cloth. "Eagles and hawks and birds of prey like that are called raptors, you know."

"Are they related to the dinosaur raptors?" Dakota wanted to know.

"Oh yes," said PaleoJoe. "It now appears that the birds and the dinosaurs are very closely related indeed. In fact, the *Utahraptor* had many similarities with our Golden Eagle friend. It had two, slender, birdlike legs, and it had keen eyesight."

"Then there was that...*hic*...special claw," said Shelly careful not to look in Cleveland's direction. She had an idea what PaleoJoe was trying to do.

"The great slasher claw," said PaleoJoe and took a large bite from his sandwich. He chewed thoughtfully a minute and then continued. "*Utahraptor* had four-toed feet and on the second toe he carried a fifteen inch sickle-like claw. *Utahraptor,* remember, is the largest and oldest known *Dromeosaurid.* It was much bigger than the small *Velociraptor. Utahraptor* was probably 20 feet in length and weighed close to a ton. He was a very impressive and a relatively smart hunter. I consider *Utahraptor* an important addition to the Raptor Exhibit at the Balboa."

PaleoJoe took a swallow of his coffee. "And that claw, Cleveland, would be a significant contribution to the exhibit. It would allow a lot of people, including scientists and scholars, to get a good view and understanding about this dinosaur."

Without a word Cleveland stood and left the picnic group. Alone he went to sit in the jeep where he pulled out his paperback and, ignoring everybody, began to read.

Owen sighed. "Nice try, PaleoJoe," he said.

PaleoJoe shrugged and finished his sandwich.

Dakota and Shelly helped Owen pack up everything making sure that they did not leave any litter behind. Then everybody piled into the jeep.

"Here we go," said Owen. "Next stop Bone Ranch!"

They began the steep journey down the cliff. At first the breeze created by the jeep traveling felt good but then Owen started to hit potholes and Dakota and Shelly and PaleoJoe were tossed around uncomfortably.

"Hey!" shouted Shelly on one particularly bad bump. The good thing, she realized, was that her

hiccups seemed to be gone, but she also thought that if she hadn't been wearing her seat belt, she could have been tossed right out of the jeep. As she looked out and down she could see that the drop was steep and dangerous.

And Owen didn't seem to be slowing down any.

In fact, he seemed to be speeding up!

"Owen! Slow down!" Cleveland yelled grabbing onto the dashboard. They were all being shaken and rattled like popcorn in a popper. "Slow down!" Cleveland shouted again. They had yet to descend most of the narrow cliff road and they were going very fast.

"I can't!" Owen yelled back. "The brakes don't work! Hang on everybody!"

Owen gripped the steering wheel and, pumping uselessly on the brakes, headed straight down Dead Man's Road out of control and going too fast.

CHAPTER TWENTY-ONE

CLEVELAND MAKES A DECISION

"Quick," yelled Dakota, almost biting his tongue as they crashed over more ruts and potholes. "Use the emergency brake!"

There is a trick you can do with emergency brakes to use them to slow down an out of control vehicle, but apparently on this jeep, Owen needed two hands to do it.

"Cleveland, take the wheel!" he shouted.

Cleveland reached over, straining against his seat belt, and grabbed onto the steering wheel. Owen worked the emergency brake and they began to slow.

Finally, as they came around the last bend of the steep road, Cleveland spotted a patch of deep loose sand and scrub. He turned the jeep into it. The drag of the sand slowed them more until, at last, they came to a bumpy stop.

"*Iguanodon* tonsils!" PaleoJoe exclaimed. "I don't ever want to do that again!"

"Me either," said Owen. He was very pale under his dark tan.

"What happened?" Cleveland demanded.

"I don't know," said Owen. "But I intend to find out."

He unbuckled his belt and leaped out of the jeep. Shelly looked over at Dakota who appeared to be sort of frozen.

"Are you okay?" she asked him.

"Huh?" It took Dakota a second to realize she was talking to him. Dakota had been wearing his sunglasses with the unreliable lens. In the bumping and tossing the lens had, of course, popped out. When he looked over at Shelly he had a strange alien look as he blinked dazedly out from one empty lens socket.

"Yes," he said. "I'm fine, but I've lost the lens on my sunglasses. It's probably somewhere back there on Dead Man's Road where it will remain until it fossilizes. And now I will have to see the world through one dark circle and one not dark circle, and the world will look silly, and I will look silly looking at the world."

Shelly didn't laugh. It had been a very close

call. "How did you know about using the emergency brake?" she asked.

"Oh, I saw Dexter North do it once in a car chase scene when someone tampered with his brakes."

"And that's what someone has done here!" Owen's angry voice came from under the hood where he had been examining things. "Someone has tampered with the brake line."

Shelly and Dakota exchanged looks. They had a pretty good idea who it had been.

"So Cleveland," said Dakota blinking at the boy through his one-lensed sunglasses. "Want to tell us about that guy you were talking to?"

"You seem to know something yourself," said Cleveland. He was pale and shaken from steering a jeep away from the edge of a cliff road. That wasn't something people asked him to do everyday. "You first."

"I'll tell him," said Shelly. And she did. She told him all about Buzzsaw, about how he had tried to steal the *Stegosaurus* eggs, how Dakota had risked his life to stop that from happening, and how Buzzsaw had now appeared again and seemed intent on sabotaging PaleoJoe's Raptor Exhibit.

While she talked, PaleoJoe borrowed her pink space age cell phone, which she always carried with her, and Owen called for someone to come and get them. Then PaleoJoe and Owen bent under the jeep hood together trying to see if they could fix the trouble

themselves. It didn't look promising.

"That's the whole story," said Shelly.

Cleveland was quiet for a bit after she had finished.

"I don't know who this Buzzsaw character is, but Dakota was right about seeing someone talking to me. I had just nipped inside the building for a minute..." Here Cleveland paused and looked a little embarrassed. "I love looking at that cliff wall. I had to go in and see it. I just didn't want you to know."

"Well," said Shelly. "It is an amazing sight. I can't blame you at all."

"So go on," said Dakota. "What happened then?"

"Well, when I came back out there was this guy walking around the jeep. When he saw me he just sort of chatted with me for a minute. I got back in the jeep and he asked me some questions about it–model and year, that sort of thing–and then he left. He was friendly enough but he had a peculiar odor about him."

"Don't I know it!" Dakota exclaimed.

"Buzzsaw is after revenge," said Shelly. "He really wants to bring down PaleoJoe and the Balboa museum. He can do it too, by discrediting them. There are all sorts of rumors flying about concerning ghosts and how the exhibit isn't safe."

"I've heard those things," said Cleveland. "That's why I didn't want to put my fossil in the museum. I didn't trust the Balboa to look after it."

"The Balboa is a safe place for fossils," said Shelly. "PaleoJoe knows what he's doing. But rumors like that can really destroy a reputation."

"Reputation is important," said Cleveland, thinking hard. "People used to call Barfield Sanders dishonest because he happened to know a couple of outlaws. But actions speak louder than words. That's something my own dad taught me and I believe it."

Cleveland looked sharply at Shelly and Dakota and then, suddenly, he grinned at them. "So if PaleoJoe wants to put my raptor claw in his exhibit, I'll let him!"

"PALEOJOE!" Shelly shrieked. PaleoJoe, startled by this sudden outburst, bumped his head on the open hood of the jeep. "Cleveland says you can have the claw!"

"That's peachy," he said rubbing his sore head and seeing flashes of bright light before his eyes. Suddenly, PaleoJoe felt the urgent need for a long shower and an even longer nap.

CHAPTER TWENTY-TWO

WHITE WATER

Eventually they were rescued by Mr. Sanders himself and rode in the air-conditioned limousine in comfort back to Bone Ranch.

"Tomorrow," said Cleveland when they were all gathered in the Fireplace Room, "I'll take you to the Outpost. We have to travel through some backcountry to get to Bone Mine. That's where I hid the raptor claw."

"Couldn't you have just hidden it under your bed?" asked Dakota.

Cleveland laughed. "Couldn't take the chance. I didn't know how good of a detective you would be, Butch." He playfully punched Dakota on the arm. Dakota retaliated by tackling him and the two rolled on the floor laughing and wrestling. Saber watched perched on the edge of the sofa, and when he saw his chance he launched himself into the tussle as well.

"Ow!" yelled Dakota. "That's claws! No fair, Saber!"

"Boys," said Shelly, rolling her eyes.

The next morning Cleveland was as good as his word. They would travel to the Outpost, which was several miles up the river through some pretty rugged country, in two groups. Owen and Dakota, with a special riding box built for Saber, would make the journey on horseback packing supplies with them. They were planning on staying at the Outpost overnight and they would need camping gear.

"Michelle Mayer and her husband Dan take care of the Outpost for us," said Mr. Sanders. "I hired them a couple of years ago. I use the Outpost as sort of a camping destination for my family and business associates when they come to visit. Michelle does most of the work. She's a wonder. I'm pretty sure that woman could fix the space shuttle if it happened to break down in her backyard. Her husband, Dan, is a journalist and so he travels all over and is gone most of the time. I already let her know you're coming. She'll have the bunks ready."

Shelly, PaleoJoe, and Cleveland were planning on making the journey by water. They would be paddling small inflatable kayaks that Cleveland called duckies.

Dakota watched them, bundled up in lifejackets, get into the strange little crafts. Shelly caught on immediately.

"Whoo-hoo!" she yelled, and did some fancy zipping around PaleoJoe who was mostly wallowing in the middle of the river.

"Use your paddle on both sides," Cleveland was calling advice to him.

Dakota shook his head. He was very glad to be going overland. He did not know how he would have been able to cope with a duckie any better than PaleoJoe. Even though Cleveland and his paddlers were supposed to reach the Outpost well ahead of them, Dakota doubted that they would get there at all unless they managed to get PaleoJoe headed in the right direction.

"Are you ready, Dakota?" asked Owen thumping Dakota on the back.

On Owen's t-shirt was a gigantic fish with a bullet shaped head and huge curved teeth. It looked stupid and slow and very dangerous.

"Hey Owen," said Dakota. "What is that on your t-shirt?"

"Ah, you noticed my dinosaur shirts, have you?" Owen smiled. "I collect them. It's a hobby. This is a *Dunkleosteus*, the largest predator in the Devonian Sea."

"I've heard of it," said Dakota. Chalk one up for Shelly, he thought.

"Come on, Butch!" said Owen swinging up into the saddle of his horse. "We're riding out of here like the Wild Bunch!"

"Yeeha!" shouted Dakota.

Dakota had ridden horses before at a camp that he had gone to one summer and so the horse he had been given to ride, a gentle mare with a brilliantly black mane and a white face, did not bother him at all. So, while Shelly splashed and shouted in the river, and PaleoJoe tried to learn to control his paddle, Owen and Dakota, with a curious Saber bundled along, rode out.

"I've got it now!" shouted PaleoJoe and it appeared that maybe he did. He had stopped going in circles and he had managed to figure out how to keep his boat, sort of, in the middle of the current and not to wander off toward the bank and water that was too shallow.

"You're looking good," Cleveland called to him. "You'll be a pro by the time we hit the white water!"

"White water?" PaleoJoe asked nervously. "Nobody said anything about any white water."

"Come on, PaleoJoe," whooped Shelly. "Last one to the outpost is a rotten *Stegosaurus* egg!"

And so they started off.

The day was brilliantly warm, but on the river it was cool and refreshing. Trees lined the banks, birds called back and forth, and insects buzzed and zoomed over the water. PaleoJoe fell a little behind the other

two, but he was getting the hang of it and by the time they reached the rapids, Cleveland had been right, he was ready for them.

The white water was really only a gentle slide through some water-smothered rocks. The river ran swift here, but it was by no means viciously fast or dangerous. And it was enormous fun.

"Yippee!" Shelly yelled and splashed her way through.

Cleveland followed.

"Yahoo!" shouted PaleoJoe and zoomed along

behind them. They rested for a few minutes in a quiet pool of calm river around the bend from the rapids.

"That was so much fun!" said Shelly. "I want to do it again only I don't know how to get back to the top."

"You'd have to hike back," said Cleveland. "You can't really paddle against the current here."

"Are there more rapids?" Shelly asked hopefully.

"Not on this stretch," said Cleveland. "The other set of rapids are past the Outpost in Calamity Canyon, but we won't be going that far. Those rapids are pretty dangerous. There's a lot more to see here, though. We're not even half way yet. Follow me!"

And so Shelly and PaleoJoe bent to their paddles.

Elsewhere on the overland trail, and well behind PaleoJoe and company, Owen was telling Dakota stories about outlaws. And Dakota was listening so intently that he failed to notice that somewhere behind them another man on a horse was following them.

CHAPTER TWENTY-THREE

MIKE

Shelly and PaleoJoe and Cleveland made it to the Outpost about an hour later. They were all pretty wet. PaleoJoe was dripping water because he had actually fallen into the river as he had tried to get out of his duckie. Shelly and Cleveland were wet because they had gotten into a splashing fight instigated by Shelly who had, most decidedly, won.

Laughing, talking, and dripping a few gallons of river water, they walked up from the river to the Outpost. The Outpost was a low, long building made from ancient timbers and looked like it had been slouching in that exact location for about a hundred years. Which it had.

"The Outpost was built by Morris Patterson, too,"

said Cleveland. "We think that Butch Cassidy stayed here once or twice when he passed through. Bone Mine, which was the old diamond mine that turned out to be a hoax, is just 5 miles west of here."

They stepped onto the wooden porch of the Outpost, deeply shaded and smelling of pine. Cleveland banged on a screen door. "Mrs. Mayer? It's Cleveland!"

He opened the door and they all trooped in. No one came to greet them. Cleveland shrugged. "I'm sure she's around here somewhere." He raised his voice and called again, "Mrs. Mayer!"

"Cleveland? Is that you?" the voice was faint and sounded muffled. "Get in here! I need some help!"

Dripping water Cleveland led the way to the kitchen. There they found a pair of tanned, knobby legs, presumably attached to a person, jutting out from an old cabinet under the sink. There was a great deal of hammering and clanking in the depths of the cabinet and then a hand appeared gesturing. "I need the wrench from over there," the muffled voice said. "You got here just in time. If I let go of this thing it will shoot water and gunk all over!"

Shelly spotted the requested wrench and gave it to the hand, which disappeared into the cabinet. There was a good deal more banging and clanging. Shelly crouched down where she could get a better view. She saw that the legs and arm belonged to a woman who was engaged in a vigorous tug of war with some sort

of monster pipe.

More banging and clanging. "There!" said the woman and scooted herself out from under the sink. Cleveland reached down a hand to help her up.

"Thanks, Sundance," said the woman brushing a long strand of hair out of her face with a grease smeared hand.

Shelly looked surprised.

"My nickname," said Cleveland, suddenly embarrassed.

"Dakota is going to get a big kick out of that!" Shelly giggled. Sundance was Butch Cassidy's sidekick. Shelly couldn't imagine anyone, especially Cleveland who was a tad bit older and a lot taller, being a sidekick for Dakota.

The woman standing next to Shelly smiled, too, making laugh lines crinkle around her friendly brown eyes. She was tall and slender and deeply tanned. Her hands, which she now wiped on a cloth from her hip pocket, were bony and looked strong. But the best thing about her, thought Shelly, was her hair. Even though it had a few strands of grey in it, it was a deep red.

"Mike? Is that you?" PaleoJoe spoke up from the doorway.

"Well, PaleoJoe!" said the woman smiling. "Of course it's me. Unless someone replaced me while I wasn't looking and that's not likely because I'm always looking!"

"It's good to see you," said PaleoJoe and gave

her a soggy hug.

"Sanders said a Paleontologist was coming," said Mike. "He didn't tell me it was you! I didn't know you could paddle a kayak!"

PaleoJoe looked a little proud, as though it had been nothing at all. He decided not to explain to Mike why he was soaking wet.

"Mike?" said Cleveland, looking a bit puzzled.

"A nickname," said the woman. "I used to be a preperator for PaleoJoe. My name is Michelle and used to be Michelle Michels until I got married. PaleoJoe called me Mike mostly because he never could remember my name."

"And a better preperator I've never met," said PaleoJoe.

"What's a preperator?" asked Cleveland.

"The person who chips the fossils out of the rock and plaster jackets and puts them on in the field," said Shelly.

"And now, Sundance, you and Miss Torch can mop up the water you've splashed all over," Mike handed the towel to Cleveland. "I always hated it when people called me Carrot Top," she said to Shelly. "Miss Torch okay with you?"

Shelly grinned. Suddenly she liked having a new nickname. It sounded like the name a superhero would have. Miss Torch. "Fine by me," she said.

It was almost dark by the time Dakota and Owen

arrived at the Outpost. By that time Miss Torch had assisted Mike in making chocolate chip cookies, and Cleveland had helped her repair two loose shingles on the roof, and PaleoJoe had been kept busy painting the back porch.

"I didn't brave all those rapids to come all this way to work," he grumbled a little bit.

But Mike was unsympathetic. "Pish, PaleoJoe," she said. "Work is good for the soul."

Immediately after meeting him, Mike started calling Dakota, Butch. She smiled at him and gave him a slap on the back that felt like he had been hit by a football player. Dakota decided that he liked Mike a lot, even though she made him go chop some wood for the evening fire. Owen helped him, but they were both sort of sore from riding horses all day and it was slow going.

Even Saber took a liking to Mike, especially after Mike gave him a pinch of catnip. Saber went into Hyperactive Ninja Cat Mode for several minutes, and when he finally paused, Mike set him up in the pantry where she kindly requested that he try to catch the mouse that was living there. Saber went right to work and later he followed Mike up onto the roof when she went to check out Cleveland's work on the shingles before it got too dark to see.

And while everyone was busy with his or her chores, Mike made a supper that ranked very high in the opinions of them all as being quite delicious.

After supper they sat out on the big front porch eating the chocolate chip cookies and talked. Soon the sky was a deep black and a brilliance of stars speckled the velvety darkness like a scattering of glitter.

"It will take us about 2 hours to get to Bone Mine," Cleveland told Shelly and Dakota.

"Wouldn't it be faster by kayak?" asked Shelly hopefully.

"Yes, it would, but it's too dangerous," said Cleveland. "Besides we have to get back out of the canyon again and I for one would not want to paddle against that current. I also wouldn't want to risk taking the fossil on the river."

"I've been wondering," said Shelly. "Why do you call it Bone Mine?"

"Is it because of all the outlaws who left their bones there when they died?" asked Dakota.

Cleveland laughed. "That's a good guess. I think, though, I'll just wait until you see it for yourselves. I can take you on a grand tour. I've explored that mine since I was a little boy. It's a dangerous place. The outlaws used it to hide in and there are booby-traps all over. Most of them are old or have been sprung but there are a few left. But you won't have to worry because I know just about every inch of the place."

"We'll stick with you then, Sundance," said Shelly.

And so, as night moved in, the Dinosaur Detective Club sat on the old porch of the Outpost and discussed

their plans for the next day. And every word they spoke
was overheard by a listener hidden in the dark.

CHAPTER TWENTY-FOUR

KIDNAPPED

Dakota was sleeping peacefully when he began to dream that he was being attacked by a pincushion. It was a red tomato looking pincushion, like the one his mother used when she was sewing, and it was poking him on his chin. The sharp little pinpricks became very real and Dakota opened his eyes to find Saber crouched on his chest using his chin as a punching bag.

"Ow! Saber, stop that!" Dakota pushed the little cat off his chest and looked at his illuminated watch. It was 2:00 in the morning. "Too early for playing, Saber. Settle down now. Sleep time."

But Saber didn't want to settle down and started marching back and forth across the mountain that was Dakota under the covers. He was trying to tell Dakota something very important, but the boy who always stuffed him in a bag seemed to be particularly deaf. Finally, Dakota rolled out of bed and escorted Saber to the hall. Dakota set him down and shut the door. Dakota was back asleep almost before he crashed onto his bed.

Shelly was dreaming about digging up a *T-Rex* fossil when a persistent soft banging and rustling suddenly awakened her. With her heart beating hard she finally discovered that the noisemaker was not a monster invading her room but Saber batting at the vinyl blinds drawn over the window.

"Saber," Shelly sighed and looked at the clock beside her bed. "It's 2:30 in the morning!" And she got up to corral Saber out of her room where, once again, the small cat found a door shut in his whiskered face.

But down the hall coming from another room the little bobtail could hear the snores of PaleoJoe...

Dakota was sound asleep and Shelly had gone back to dreams of other dinosaur discoveries when everyone was shocked awake by the crashing and beating of pots and pans. Dakota sat bolt upright in bed, his hair standing on end, and Shelly thought maybe the whole house was caving in as she catapulted out of her room in search of the wild noise.

It was Mike and she was standing in the kitchen beating on a frying pan with a small saucepan.

"Mike!" PaleoJoe, never in the sweetest temper in the morning, until after he had had his coffee, looked particularly dangerous as he staggered in, his eyes still blurry with sleep, his hair a shaggy uncombed mess.

"Good," said Mike clanging her pots down on the table. "You're all here. I'm not apologizing for the noise because we have an emergency."

"What emergency?" demanded Owen. Owen looked like a refugee from a zombie convention with his long dark hair a great tangle around his head. He was wearing an oversized *Stegosaurus* t-shirt full of holes.

"Cleveland has been kidnapped," said Mike.

"What!!?" everybody pretty much said together.

"That's right," said Mike. "Saber–he's an extremely intelligent young cat you know–woke me up a few minutes ago and I realized that something was wrong right away. I found out the kitchen door had been forced opened and I discovered that Cleveland is missing."

Dakota bent down to find Saber crouched under the kitchen table very proud of himself to have, at last, managed to wake everybody, but not at all liking the noise Mike had been making.

"So that's what all the pin poking was about," said Dakota. Saber blinked at him.

"How do you know he didn't just leave or go for a walk or something?" asked Shelly.

"One, it's 4:30 in the morning and Cleveland

hates to get up early, let alone when it is still mostly night and two, if you take a look in his bedroom you will see that there must have been a huge struggle."

Quickly, PaleoJoe led the way to Cleveland's room and it was just like Mike said. Bedding was tossed and twisted on the floor, a chair lay on its side and a small table lamp lay broken in a corner.

"Oh, and one of the horses is gone too," said Mike.

"It's Buzzsaw," said Dakota.

"Let's not jump to conclusions here," said Owen.

"No, Owen," said Shelly. "I'm sure Dakota is right."

"So am I," said PaleoJoe. "I think Buzzsaw has taken Cleveland to the Bone Mine to get the *Utahraptor* fossil. This is serious."

"There's one way to find out," said Owen and he dashed back to the kitchen where he found a flashlight. He ran outside and was gone for several minutes. When he came back he confirmed their fears.

"You can see fresh horse tracks up the trail leading to Bone Mine," he said.

"Okay then," said PaleoJoe. "Owen, you and I will go after them. Mike, get hold of Richard Sanders and tell him what has happened. He can get some law up here. Shelly, you and Dakota stay here."

"No problem," said Shelly cooperatively. Dakota gave her a surprised look. It wasn't like Shelly to agree so easily to stay out of the action. It made him a bit nervous.

It was the work of mere minutes for Owen and PaleoJoe to throw on some clothes and saddle the remaining horses. Inside Mike was busy trying to contact Cleveland's dad. Dakota and Shelly stood on the porch watching as PaleoJoe and Owen rode off into the darkness of the trail.

"You agreed to stay behind awful easily," said Dakota.

"That's because we aren't going to stay behind," said Shelly. "I have a plan."

"Of course you do," said Dakota, suddenly wishing he could just go back to bed. Shelly's plans seemed to always involve danger.

"Can you swim?" she asked him.

"About as well as I can fly," said Dakota.

"Well, it won't be too bad," said Shelly. "You'll be wearing a life preserver."

"Why would I be wearing a life preserver?" asked Dakota, suddenly fearful of what Shelly had in mind.

"Because," said Shelly, "we're going to get to the mine via the river and we will have to go through Calamity Canyon to do it!"

CHAPTER TWENTY-FIVE

CALAMITY CANYON

The sky was beginning to pale into dawn as Shelly and Dakota launched the duckies into the river.

"I'm pretty sure this is a bad idea," said Dakota, as he tried to figure out how to stop paddling in a circle.

"Cleveland is going to need help," said Shelly. "PaleoJoe and Owen will get there too only we'll get there a bit ahead of them and help Cleveland sooner. Here, paddle like this." And Shelly demonstrated.

Fortunately, Dakota was an athletic boy and had good coordination. He caught on quickly and the two set off skimming over the quiet dawn water of the river.

If they hadn't been paddling swiftly toward

danger, Dakota might have enjoyed the coolness of dawn as it came sliding over the river waking up the birds and lighting the cottonwood and willows along the banks. After about a half hour of swift gliding a cliff began to enclose the river and the trees disappeared.

"We must be entering Calamity Canyon," said Shelly. "The rapids should be somewhere just ahead."

The cliff walls rose tall on either side of Shelly and Dakota. The river narrowed. Soon it was like paddling through a corridor. The cliff walls were pale and quite beautiful as the morning light began to penetrate into the shaded protection of the cliff face. Suddenly, as the morning light slid down the canyon walls, strange figures and marks began to appear.

"Hey, what's that?" asked Dakota, pointing to the face of the cliff. He watched in fascination as the dawn light began to reveal strange drawings carved into the rock face.

Etched into the surface of the rock were bizarre figures shaped like trapezoids. Small square heads rested on top of the trapezoid shaped bodies and thin carved lines representing arms and legs extended out from this. Some of the figures seemed to be carrying shields bearing a spiral design or rays like small suns. The figures seemed to be about two to four feet tall and as Dakota and Shelly drifted closer they could make out other details on the figures like belts, extra arms, and small poked holes that could represent necklaces.

"Wow!" said Shelly. "I think those are petroglyphs. Mike told me a little bit about them yesterday when we were making cookies."

"Who made them?" asked Dakota. "And why would they put them here in the middle of a canyon?"

"Mike said most of them were made by the Fremont Indians. They were a farming culture in this state about 800 years ago. No one really knows what the art work means, though. Mike said she would show me some sometime. This is really amazing!"

Dakota had to agree but just then he could feel his duckie begin to pick up speed, and now he could also hear the sound of rushing, gulping water. "Look out, Shelly," he yelled. "White water!"

He was right. The kayaks rounded the bend of the canyon and shot out into a frothy jumble of violent water. Dakota didn't have any time for thinking. He could only react. The river seemed to disappear into a boiling and churning mass of roaring water as Dakota was shot forward like one of those water park rides, only there wasn't any nice and sturdy metal chute to guide him along.

Over the thunder and boom of the rambunctious water Dakota thought he heard Shelly yell "Whoo-hoo!" but he couldn't spare a minute. Water slapped him in the face splashing vigorously all around him. Dakota fought to keep from turning over. He rode through the raging water bobbing like a cork in a monster maelstrom until, all at once, he found himself skimming out of the thunderous surging water into a section of calm current.

The cliff walls were behind him now–or actually they were in front of him because Dakota had emerged from his white water ride going backwards. Turning his kayak around, Dakota saw Shelly already paddling toward the bank. He also saw the amazing building, which rested in a clump of cottonwood not far from the river. It was a small cabin resting in the scant shade of the trees and it appeared to be made of bones.

Swiftly, Dakota followed Shelly and the two of them drew their kayaks out of the river securing them out of reach of the water. Together they scrambled up the bank and quietly, keeping low so as not to be seen, they began to sneak up toward the cabin.

"Dakota," Shelly gasped as they got closer. "I think that cabin is made of dinosaur bones!"

"Pretty cool, isn't it, little girl," said a snide and sneery voice from directly behind them.

Dakota and Shelly whirled around to find themselves face to face with Buzzsaw.

CHAPTER TWENTY-SIX

THE CABIN OF BONES

"Come on inside and let me show you around," said Buzzsaw as though Dakota and Shelly were friends, and as though they would really want to go anywhere with Buzzsaw.

"How's it going, Spike?" Buzzsaw asked and then, reaching out, he grabbed Dakota's arm and twisted it up behind his back.

"Ow!" yelped Dakota.

"I invited you inside, Spike. Where are your manners?"

And so, even though they didn't want to, they really had no choice and Buzzsaw escorted them inside the cabin. Sunlight filtered through the walls of the cabin that were, just as Shelly said, made from dinosaur bones. Dakota thought there must be about a million of them. They were all sizes from the massive leg bones of Sauropods to smaller teeth like bones, ribs, and parts of skulls.

"Thought you two would show up sooner or later," said Buzzsaw, as he shoved Dakota down onto a rickety old chair. "No sign of PaleoJoe though. What happened to him? Did he drown in the river?"

"We aren't going to tell you anything," said Shelly, with some spirit.

"Where's Cleveland?" Dakota demanded.

"The rich kid is up at the mine," said Buzzsaw. "He's getting something for me. Now, Miss Know-It -All Big Nose, have a seat over here."

He gabbed Shelly's arm and roughly sat her down on another old chair that wobbled under her sudden weight. Dakota thought about maybe tackling Buzzsaw when he wasn't looking, but he didn't want to do it while Buzzsaw had hold of Shelly. He was afraid that Shelly might get hurt.

And then he lost his chance. Buzzsaw had produced a roll of duct tape and he was securing Shelly to the chair by binding her hands behind the chair back.

"This is a pretty cool place isn't it?" said Buzzsaw conversationally. "Rich boy tells me it was built by an outlaw with talent. Sounds like someone I would like!" He laughed. It was a harsh and mean laugh.

"Buzzsaw, PaleoJoe is right behind us," said

141

Shelly. "He has about 50 police officers with him. You won't get away with this!"

Buzzsaw finished with Shelly and started on Dakota who swiftly got the same treatment with the duct tape.

"This cabin could be your vacation spot," Buzzsaw taunted them. "I would think, Miss Carrot-Top Paleontologist, that you would be very happy here. Enjoy your stay." And then he left leaving behind an unattractive whiff of *Viking Vitamin Drops*.

"*Grrr,*" Shelly growled sounding a bit like Saber. She struggled against the tape, rocking and bouncing in her chair. "He called me Carrot-Top! Just wait until I get out of here. That stinky coprolite will wish he had never ever met me!"

A coprolite, Dakota knew, was fossilized dinosaur poop, and, for that matter, Buzzsaw probably already wished he had never met Shelly or Dakota. But, all in all, he very much agreed with Shelly on this one.

Dakota struggled against the tape on his arms. Once before Buzzsaw had secured him to a chair and Dakota had thought that it would be an experience he would never have to repeat. He wasn't thrilled about being wrong.

After several minutes of struggling Shelly stopped to catch her breath and began to look around at the cabin interior.

"This really is an amazing place," she said.

Besides the two rickety chairs there was an old

table tilted on its side. The interior was dim, but light poked through openings between the bones where the mud of whatever material had originally been used a long time ago had now worn away.

"I wonder how they managed to build it," said Shelly.

"And I wonder how we're going to get out of it," said Dakota, experimentally bouncing his chair up and down. He thought that maybe he could break it. But the chair appeared to be made stronger than it looked.

"We'll think of something," said Shelly, realizing her hands were beginning to go numb from lack of circulation. And then an instant later she saw something that gave her an idea. "Hey, Dakota..."

"Right here," said Dakota. "I haven't gone anywhere on account of this smelly guy who taped me to this chair."

Shelly ignored this sarcasm. "I think I can see a fragment of bone jutting out of the wall just a little behind you. It looks like it's sharp, maybe splintered or something. Maybe you could use it to saw through the tape."

"Good idea," said Dakota craning his neck around trying to see what Shelly had spotted. "I don't see it."

"It's right there," Shelly pointed with her chin. "Just behind your right shoulder."

Dakota craned around and, of course, craned too far and tipped himself over. He went crashing down.

143

The back of his head hit the dirt floor of the cabin with a slightly hollow sounding *thunk* and made him dizzy for a second.

"Are you okay?" asked Shelly anxiously.

"Peachy," croaked Dakota, the breath momentarily knocked out of him. He wondered if he had knocked himself out and then realized he wouldn't be wondering that if he had. And then his attention focused on the ceiling of the cabin.

"Hey, Shelly..." he said.

"Right here, Butch," Shelly answered.

"Do you think you would recognize that claw thing of Cleveland's if you saw it?"

"The fossil? Of course. Why?"

"Because I think I'm looking at it," said Dakota.

CHAPTER TWENTY-SEVEN

BONE MINE

"Where?" asked Shelly eagerly looking around.

"Up there in the ceiling," said Dakota. "It's lodged between those two other bones."

Shelly looked up. "Yes! I see it too!" And she got so carried away squirming with excitement at this discovery that she, too, went crashing to the floor.

"Ow," she said. "I hope I didn't break my arm! But on the bright side, I've got a better view now." She lay there feeling bruised, her arms, not broken, still slowly going numb. Shelly didn't pay any attention to that. She was completely fascinated by the bones she was looking at.

"It's definitely the claw of the *Utahraptor*," she informed Dakota. "I can also see some bones that look like the lower jaw of maybe a *Diplodocus*. There's a

145

rib or two of something...oh, some vertebrate bone... femurs...Wow, I wish PaleoJoe were here. He would know what all those bones are."

"I wish PaleoJoe were here, too," Dakota grunted with the effort of scooting himself over to the bit of bone Shelly had spotted earlier. He managed to get himself scrunched up against it. He began to saw away at the tough tape that held his wrists together. As Shelly continued to make her catalog of ceiling bones, Dakota finally managed to free himself.

"Thank goodness," said Shelly, rubbing her arms and hands with relief after Dakota had freed her. Her arms were prickling as the blood began to circulate once again.

"How long do you think it will be before PaleoJoe and Owen get here?" asked Dakota.

"I don't know," said Shelly. "But I don't think we can wait, do you?

"Well yes, actually I do," said Dakota, but he was talking to Shelly's back as she was already leaving the cabin of bones.

"The mine has to be around here somewhere," she said over her shoulder.

Actually the mine was pretty easy to find. The opening to it was hidden just behind a small hill at the back of the cabin. A few boards that had covered the entrance lay on the ground nearby. Cautiously, Shelly and Dakota crept closer and peered inside the dark opening.

The air from the old mine smelled like earth and was damp and cool. From somewhere out of sight, they could hear the faint sound of voices.

"It's Buzzsaw," said Shelly, after a few seconds of listening hard. "He must be talking to Cleveland."

"Good, then Cleveland is okay and we should just wait here for PaleoJoe," said Dakota.

"Of course we can't," said Shelly. "At any moment Buzzsaw could discover that the fossil is not hidden in the mine. He could get mad at Cleveland for lying to him and he could hurt him. Listen!"

Dakota listened. He could hear the hum of insects in the scrubby grass around the mine entrance and he could hear the faint murmur of voices from within.

"I don't think they are very deep inside," said Shelly. "Come on. Follow me."

"Sure," said Dakota reluctantly, as Shelly started forward into the mine. "I'm sure glad you can see in the dark because I'm pretty sure I can't."

Out of the bright light, the mine interior was dark and the first thing Shelly did was to step on a rock and turn her ankle.

"Oh!" she gasped.

Dakota reached out to steady her. Then they both held their breaths wondering if they had been heard.

But the distant murmur of voices continued uninterrupted.

"Ow!" whispered Shelly fiercely, rubbing her ankle.

147

"Are you okay?" asked Dakota.

"Yes, I'm fine," said Shelly. "Stupid rock!" And she kicked it. It went skittering into the darkness and for a moment the voices stopped. Shelly and Dakota froze. There was nowhere to hide.

"Oops," said Shelly.

But no one came to investigate the noise and after several seconds the voices resumed.

By now Dakota's eyes were adjusted to the gloom

"Follow me," he said taking the lead. "And please, no more rock soccer, okay?"

He led them deeper into the mine and just when it was going to get too dark to see, Dakota spotted a glow from lights just ahead. Moving cautiously forward, Dakota became aware of a large pile of rubble that partially blocked the passageway into the area brightly lit by the lights. Moving carefully ahead of Shelly he approached the pile of rubble and crouched down behind it. He motioned Shelly forward. Shelly crouched and crawled down next to him. Cautiously she peered over Dakota's shoulder to see what he was spying on.

It was a small open chamber. Several battery operated lanterns lit the walls with a yellowish light. Scattered about were dozens of wooden crates. They were old. The wood was partially rotted and they were all covered with a thin layer of dirt that had sifted down upon them over the long years. But Shelly stifled a gasp when she saw what was inside the crates.

Bones!

And that wasn't all. The walls of the mine here were studded with bones. They emerged from the rock face in a hodgepodge jumble just like the bones on the cliff wall at Dinosaur National Monument.

Now Shelly understood why it was called Bone Mine. Old Barfield Sanders had expected to find diamonds and instead his men kept digging up bones. There had been so many of them that they had built a whole cabin of them. And, in those days, they probably did not understand what it was they had found. Not diamonds, not coal, just a whole lot of massive, strange bones.

Buzzsaw was standing in front of Cleveland scowling.

"If you hid it, you should be able to find it!" he was saying in a harsh and angry voice.

"I know, I know," said Cleveland sounding helpless. "But I can't remember exactly where I put it. I mean look at all these boxes. It could be anywhere really."

"Find it," said Buzzsaw threateningly. "Find it now."

And of course that's when Shelly decided to sneeze. She tried to muffle it, but it was no use. Quick as a striking snake Buzzsaw jumped around the fallen pile of rubble and had Dakota by his neck and Shelly by her ponytail and no one could do a thing about it.

"Ow!" shrieked Shelly. She hated to have her hair pulled, and Buzzsaw was pulling so hard she thought he might pull her ponytail right off.

"AK!" gasped Dakota who was finding it hard to breathe with Buzzsaw's strong hand clamped on his neck. He was pinned against the wall and he couldn't move.

"Let them go," demanded Cleveland.

Buzzsaw laughed. It wasn't a nice laugh either. "You two just don't give up, do you?" He shook Dakota and twisted his fist tighter into Shelly's hair. She was standing on tiptoe now and tears were starting in her eyes with the pain of having her hair pulled.

Buzzsaw flung Dakota to the ground where he lay gasping for breath. Then Buzzsaw tossed Shelly at Cleveland as though she were nothing but a rag doll. She went crashing into Cleveland who caught her and steadied her.

"Help rich boy find the fossil," he told her. "I don't have all day and neither does he." And he reached down once again grabbing Dakota by his neck. Dakota tried to squirm free, but Buzzsaw kneeled on his chest and squeezed until Dakota stopped struggling.

"Okay," said Cleveland. "Stop hurting Dakota. We'll find it."

Cleveland gave Shelly a desperate look. They both knew that the fossil wasn't here in the mine. What were they going to do?

CHAPTER TWENTY-EIGHT

THE TRAP

Dakota, sprawled once again on his back, endured the smelly weight of Buzzsaw. He was beginning to formulate a plan. Several feet up in the dim ceiling of the lit chamber, Dakota was observing a curious thing. Mostly camouflaged among the rafters of the tunnel, it looked like a huge canvas sling, and it seemed to hold a lot of something heavy. Maybe, rocks. But, it was obviously very old and connected to it was a bit of fraying rope. As Dakota studied the sling-like contraption and tried not to think about suffocating, if Buzzsaw decided to squeeze his neck again, he began to realize that what he was looking at was the remains of one of the old booby-traps Cleveland had been telling him about.

The question now was, was this a trap that Cleveland had disabled or was it still in working condition?

Dakota traced the rope with his eyes and discovered that the end of it disappeared near one of the crates close to Cleveland.

"*Ak–uk,*" Dakota tried to speak and Buzzsaw tightened his grip.

"Are you trying to say something, Spike?" Buzzsaw asked smiling meanly. "Go ahead. We're listening."

"Cleveland," Dakota gasped as Buzzsaw slightly loosened his grip. "PaleoJoe will be on you like a *ton of bricks* if you give that fossil to Buzzsaw."

Cleveland paused for a minute and looked hard at Dakota. He had caught the emphasis in Dakota's words. He was puzzling it out. Dakota stared back.

"And I wonder who cares about that, Spike?" Buzzsaw said and gave a mean chuckle, but Dakota watched Cleveland's eyes flick to the ceiling and then quickly away. Cleveland gave a slight nod. He understood.

"PaleoJoe will never get my fossil," said Cleveland. "He can have one of these other ones if he wants. But not mine!"

Buzzsaw laughed. "That's the spirit, rich boy."

"Well really, Buzzsaw," said Shelly brushing her hands on her shorts. She was quick to take up her cue. She had seen the look that passed between the boys.

She would do her part. "There are enough other fossils here that would do just as well. Why don't you take one of them instead? Like, I mean, take a look at this one," and she held up a long tapering bone that was clearly very heavy. She staggered a bit with the weight of it and then tripped in such a way that she sort of lunged directly at Buzzsaw.

Angrily, Buzzsaw had to release Dakota as he swatted away the heavy bone that was being propelled toward his stomach.

And the rest happened very quickly.

Dakota rolled to one side to miss both Shelly's bone and to try and get away from Buzzsaw. Cleveland made a lunge for the end of the rope Dakota had seen and pulled.

There was a moment when nothing happened and then the sling released its contents on top of Buzzsaw.

Bones.

The sling had been filled with bones. Big bones.

Unfortunately, Buzzsaw was able to throw himself backwards and so the bones missed him completely.

But maybe the ceiling that came caving in after the bones hadn't. At least, after he got done coughing and wheezing, Dakota hoped that Buzzsaw hadn't escaped. There had been a great rumbling and rushing sound as tons of dirt and rock rained down. A great cloud of choking dirt filled the chamber. Cleveland and Shelly had covered their heads with their arms and ducked for cover.

When it was over Dakota discovered that he and Shelly and Cleveland were effectively sealed in the mine. Buzzsaw was either under the cave in or on the other side.

"Is everyone okay?" Cleveland asked, helping Shelly to her feet.

"I'm fine," said Shelly irritably. "Just next time you intend to pull down the ceiling a little warning might be nice. Are you okay Dakota?"

"Peachy," croaked Dakota. He coughed. He had gritty dirt in his mouth and he was pretty sure his windpipe had been crushed.

"Spike? If you can hear me, give this message to PaleoJoe." It was Buzzsaw. His voice came through the wall of cave-in muffled, but angry sounding. "He hasn't heard the last of me!"

And then there was silence…too much silence.

"I guess it's no use to hope that he's gone for help," said Cleveland.

"It will be okay," said Shelly. "PaleoJoe and Owen should be here soon. They'll find us."

"If we don't run out of air first," said Cleveland.

"Peachy," said Dakota.

CHAPTER TWENTY-NINE

THE BALBOA CURSE

It was only about a half an hour later that Shelly heard voices calling. She and Dakota and Cleveland yelled themselves hoarse, but were able to alert PaleoJoe and Owen to their location. Then they had to wait some more while a bunch of people dug them out.

Dakota had never been happier to see daylight in his entire life. He was covered from head to foot with dirt, but then so were Shelly and Cleveland. They all looked like an episode of Invasion of the Sand People. Owen had canteens of fresh water for them, which they gulped down. Then they went splashing in the river to clean off.

Later that evening they gathered once again at the Outpost. Mike was there with Saber, Mr.

155

Sanders was there with the chief of police, and Shelly, Dakota, and Cleveland told their story. When they were finished, Cleveland brought out something big and heavy wrapped in brown paper. He handed it to PaleoJoe.

"I realize," said Cleveland, "that Buzzsaw has been making things very difficult for you and your museum. I know now that it had nothing to do with you. So I would like it very much if you would accept this fossil to put on display in your Raptor exhibit for as long as you want."

Carefully, PaleoJoe reached into the bag and pulled out the *Utahraptor* killer claw fossil. "It will be an honor," said PaleoJoe.

"And there is just one other thing," said Mike. She was sitting in a rocking chair with a chubby Saber purring contentedly on her knee. "I understand that this small, and very intelligent cat, needs a home."

Dakota felt a lump begin to grow in his throat. "That's true," he said.

"I would like to adopt him," said Mike. "I would give him a good home, Butch. And you can come and visit him anytime you want."

Dakota could only nod. He knew it was the best thing for Saber, but he also knew that Utah was very far away from his home and that the chances of visiting his bobtailed friend were very remote.

A few days later PaleoJoe, Shelly and Dakota

were ready to return home. Mr. Sanders had his private jet ready to fly them back. Shelly was very excited about flying in such comfort. PaleoJoe didn't mind it either. He thought maybe he could get used to traveling in this way pretty easily, especially when Owen informed him that the plane had been stocked with PaleoJoe's favorite coffee–mocha with a dash of almond and raspberry.

Only Dakota was sad. His backpack felt empty and lifeless. He missed Saber very much indeed.

It had been decided that Cleveland would return with them so he could assist in installing his fossil in the display. He also wanted to see the Raptor Room for himself.

It seemed to be a short and easy flight. When the plane touched down at last, PaleoJoe was surprised to see Detective Franks in the terminal waiting for them.

"Hi PaleoJoe," Detective Franks greeted them. "I hear you folks had a little excitement on your trip."

"Just a little, Du Concombre," said Shelly grinning. "We managed to cope though."

Detective Franks smiled at her. "Well, I'm sorry to have to tell you this, PaleoJoe, but there has been more trouble at the museum." And he handed PaleoJoe a newspaper.

It was the frontpage story. MUSEUM CURSE TO CLOSE DOWN RAPTOR EXHIBIT. It had been written by June Pierceson.

An insider at the Balboa Museum of Natural History has confirmed the possibility of the closing

of the much anticipated Raptor Exhibit scheduled to open later this week. Due to the continued vandalism occurring in the Exhibit, the museum source said, the Exhibit would be dismantled and would not open as advertised.

PaleoJoe, the Balboa Paleontologist responsible for the exhibit, was unavailable for comment, but other sources say there is a curse at work in the Balboa. How else could the vandalism be taking place? Police detectives have been unable to discover anyone responsible for the damage. Detective Theodore Franks stated Monday that review of surveillance tapes had turned up no evidence of human interference.

PaleoJoe looked up from the paper. "Who is this museum insider?" he asked.

"I don't know," said Detective Franks. "But I do know I didn't give the paper any official statement."

"Well, come on," said PaleoJoe. "The Exhibit is supposed to open tomorrow. We'd better get to the Balboa and figure this out."

So PaleoJoe and Detective Franks headed for the museum and on the way they dropped off Shelly and Dakota at their homes. Cleveland went with Dakota. "I'll call you if anything happens," PaleoJoe promised Shelly.

Suspiciously, Dakota thought, Shelly seemed fine with that.

It had been decided that Cleveland would stay with Dakota and so the two boys were watching TV and eating pizza when Dakota got a phone call from Shelly.

"Dakota, we've got to do something to help PaleoJoe," said Shelly urgently.

"Well, I agree," said Dakota, chomping on a piece of double cheese pepperoni pizza with black olives. "What do you suggest?"

"I have a plan," said Shelly.

"Oh no," said Dakota feeling a little surge of panic in his stomach. "Not another one of your plans."

"Let me talk to Cleveland," said Shelly.

Reluctantly Dakota handed Cleveland the phone. "Don't let her talk you into anything," he said.

Cleveland put the phone to his ear and listened. "Uh-huh," he said. "Yeah...sure...yep...uh-huh. Good plan. See you then." He gave the phone back to Dakota.

"Good plan?" said Dakota.

"Sure, Butch," Cleveland grinned. "Can you sneak us out of here, without your mom knowing, it around 8:30?"

Dakota sighed. He had a feeling it was going to be a long night.

CHAPTER THIRTY

SHELLY'S PLAN

Dakota and Cleveland met Shelly on the front steps of the Balboa museum at 8:50 that night. It was a Thursday night and on Thursdays the museum stayed open until 9:00 p.m.

"Okay, here's the plan," said Shelly. "We are going to go inside the museum and then we are going to hide."

"Hide where?" asked Dakota.

"When the museum closes we are going to sneak out and cover the Raptor Exhibit," Shelly continued, ignoring him.

"Cover it how?" asked Dakota. He was beginning to feel a little desperate.

"We are then going to guard the Exhibit..."

"Especially my claw," said Cleveland.

"How are we going to guard the Exhibit?" asked Dakota.

"And we are either going to catch Buzzsaw in the act of vandalism..." said Shelly.

"Or we are going to get first hand experience of a curse in action," said Dakota.

"That's the spirit!" said Cleveland pounding him on the back. "Get it? Spirit?" He laughed. "Sometimes I crack myself up," he said.

"Come on," said Shelly. "Let's go."

Think *Mission Impossible*, Dakota said to himself. Yeah right, he thought, impossible being the operative word.

Shelly, it turned out, had thought it through. She led Dakota and Cleveland into the museum and managed to get them all to the third floor without being spotted by Gamma Brooks, Annie the museum secretary, PaleoJoe, who was standing in the atrium of all places, or even Bob, the maintenance chief, whom they glimpsed as they scurried past the second floor. Bob had been headed toward the Raptor Room carrying his toolbox obviously going to fix something else that had been broken, Dakota thought.

"So where are we going to hide?" asked Dakota.

"THE MUSEUM IS NOW CLOSING. WILL EVERYONE PLEASE MAKE THEIR WAY TO THE ATRIUM AND MAIN DOORS." Shelly recognized

her Gamma Brook's voice making the announcement.

"Follow me," said Shelly.

Quickly she led them into the Throckmorton Rock and Mineral Room. Alfred Throckmorton was the wealthy lumber baron who had endowed the Balboa Museum back in 1925 when the museum had first been constructed. An avid world traveler, the Balboa housed several of Mr. Throckmorton's somewhat eccentric collections. The Rock and Mineral Room was one of them.

Now, as the museum was closing, the room, never the most popular of places to view, was completely deserted.

"They check all the rooms as they turn off the lights," Dakota pointed out. "They will find us in here because there isn't any place for us to hide."

It was true. The room was bare except for the glass cases containing the rocks and minerals.

"We aren't staying here," said Shelly. Out of her pocket she took a key. "I borrowed this from PaleoJoe," she said. Dakota suspected that what Shelly had done was one of the famous Borrows that Dakota himself had, on occasion, indulged in. After meeting PaleoJoe and Detective Franks, however, Dakota had absolutely stopped practicing Borrowing. With a sinking heart, Dakota wondered if he was a bad influence on Shelly.

Shelly led them to a door at the far end of the room. Using the key, she unlocked it and they stepped inside. Shelly closed and locked the door behind them.

They were standing in a pitch and musty smelling dark. Shelly and Cleveland flicked on flashlights.

"Peachy," said Dakota. "How come nobody told me to bring a flashlight?"

"Come on," said Shelly. Following the unsteady dancing swirl of the flashlights, Dakota tripped along behind Shelly and Cleveland to the foot of an iron spiral staircase. Shelly shone her flashlight up into a high dark depth.

"After you," said Cleveland.

"Where is this?" asked Dakota.

"We are going to hide up there in the old research library on the fourth floor," said Shelly. "No one ever goes up there, except during the day, and most people don't use it at all anymore because they use the Internet for research."

She started up the spiral staircase. Dakota came next with Cleveland bringing up the rear.

"No one ever checks here because the door is always locked," said Shelly her voice sounding hollow as she advanced up the spiral. "Besides, this is where Barnabus Johnson is supposed to hang out and no one wants to run into him late at night. Come on, Dakota. We're almost there!"

The research library was dusty and smelled like old leather with a mustiness that made Dakota sneeze. Library stacks of books created long corridors through the room, standing in eerie silence. And it was dark.

Shelly led the way to the back and down one

long corridor of books to the very end. There, a small study table was pushed against the wall. Shelly put her backpack on it. She shone her light on the books in the nearby stacks.

"Look," she said. "Here's a book called *The Bone Wars*. That looks interesting."

"Come on, focus here, Shelly," said Dakota nervously. "Are you sure no one will find us here?"

"Absolutely," said Shelly. "There are no windows here so no one will see our lights. And no one ever comes up here anyway."

At least no one living, thought Dakota.

Shelly dug into her pink backpack and produced a supply of candy bars. Dakota felt a little better when she handed him some beef jerky.

And there, gathered around the little study table looking at old and dusty paleontology books, they waited until midnight.

"Bob and Mr. Summers do a last security round at 11:00," said Shelly. "They are finished by 11:30 and then they go home. There is a security guard that stays on the main floor all night, but he doesn't patrol or anything. He just sits in the office area and scans the security cameras."

"How do you know all this?" asked Cleveland.

"Shelly practically lives in this museum," said Dakota.

Shelly giggled. "But this is the first time I've ever spent the night in it."

From her backpack Shelly produced one of the museum maps given out at the front desk. On it she had marked the locations of the security cameras.

"For the most part," she said, "if we crawl along the floor close to the walls, the cameras can't see us. The trick will be the long Trilobite Balcony to the Special Exhibits Room. We can crawl, but then we have to wait and time it until the camera pans away because on the back side of its sweep it has a full view of the end of the Trilobite Balcony. Somebody could see us if they are looking."

"What do we do when we get there?" asked Dakota. "Are we going to hide in the Raptor Room?"

"Nope," said Shelly carefully refolding her map. "We're going to hide in the *Megatherium.*"

CHAPTER THIRTY-ONE

THE VANDAL

"All three of us?" Dakota couldn't believe it. How could all three of them fit inside the giant sloth?

"Come on," said Shelly. "It's time to move out. Oh, and don't touch the bars on any of the windows or you will set off the security alarms. Follow me."

Quietly they descended the iron spiral staircase and Shelly let them out into the Mineral Room. The museum was eerily quiet and dim. The Mineral Room was dully lit by a couple of display lights, but otherwise the room was dark and shadowy.

Shelly led the way out. They couldn't risk using the elevator and so they took the stairs, walking quietly and staying close to the walls. These stairs were old like the ones going down to the Tombs, but they were carpeted and so they didn't squeak and creak so much.

On the second floor they paused at the foot of the stairs. A red Exit sign glowed above their heads. Dim security lights lighted Dinosaur Hall and the shadows of the great skeletons seemed almost real in the extreme silence. Dakota looked hard at the *Stegosaurus* just a few feet away. It seemed to be looking at him out of bony eye sockets. He wanted to make sure that it wasn't moving.

Shelly, who didn't suffer from an overactive imagination, looked alertly around and then led them quickly to the Trilobite Balcony. Silently she pointed out the camera. They watched it as it panned through its viewing arc. It was going to be like timing a dash through a sprinkler, thought Dakota. Something he was never very good at.

Suddenly, Shelly dropped to her hands and knees. The other two followed her example. Quickly they crawled the length of the balcony keeping just below the edges of the trilobite display cases. They paused when they reached the end of the camera's blind spot. Now they would have to wait and time it just right or they would be seen.

Shelly looked back over her shoulder carefully observing the camera. "Get ready," she whispered. "On my signal, move fast and don't trip."

Dakota hastily glanced at his shoes to make sure his laces were tied.

"NOW!" said Shelly.

Crab-like the three scuttled the rest of the length

of the balcony and dived around the corner piling up under the feet of the towering *Megatherium.*

"Come on," said Shelly. "Inside."

Amazingly, they all three fit inside. Of course Dakota had Cleveland's elbow in his ribcage and Shelly's ponytail in his face, but other than that it was quite comfortable.

Shelly had Dakota's knee in her gut and she was pretty sure that if she moved at all she would squash Cleveland. It was like playing Sardines, the game where you tried to see how many people you could stuff in a small car or a phone booth or a small cupboard. Or a *Megatherium.*

"This is quite fun," said Dakota. "We should do this more often."

"Quiet you *Trachodon,*" said Shelly irritably.

"That means Duckbilled dinosaur," Dakota informed Cleveland. "She's called me that before."

"I hope we don't have to stay like this too long," Cleveland grunted.

It was really stuffy and a bit hard to breathe.

"Can you see anything?" asked Shelly urgently.

The *Megatherium* was actually quite an elderly exhibit. He hadn't been retouched or repaired in about 30 years. Cleveland was peering out a very small opening that had, over time, formed just under the *Megatherium's* left arm, the one that was raised in the air as though the creature were reaching for a tree branch.

"Just a little," said Cleveland. "Wait! Hang on. Someone is coming!"

Through his unlikely spy hole Cleveland could just see the figure of a man stealthily approaching the door to the Raptor Room. Apparently unconcerned about the security camera, the man paused and Cleveland could see that he was carrying a crowbar.

Uh-oh, thought Cleveland. A person could do a lot of damage with a crowbar.

The man opened the door to the Raptor Room and stepped inside closing the door behind him.

"Someone just went into the Raptor Room," said Cleveland urgently. "Shelly, he had a crowbar!"

"Come on," said Shelly. "Let's get out of here. We have to stop him!"

"Oof," said Dakota as Shelly sort of punched him in the stomach in her haste to tumble from the *Megatherium*.

The three crawled and tumbled from their hiding place.

"Look," said Shelly pointing down the balcony to the security camera. It now hung lifeless, pointing down at the floor. "He's disabled the security camera."

She marched up to the doors of the Raptor Room.

"Shelly, no!" Dakota grabbed her arm and hung on firmly. "Barging will NOT work here. You don't know who is in there and Cleveland says he has a crowbar."

"That's right," said Cleveland. "Someone could get hurt."

"So what do we do?" asked Shelly in frustration.

Dakota thought quickly. "I have an idea," he said.

The man stood inside the Raptor Room and looked around, a dark scowl on his face. He hefted the crowbar in his hand and considered what he had come to do. In a way, he hated to destroy something as valuable as the *Utahraptor* claw, but a quarter of a million dollars was a lot of money. That's what Buzzsaw had offered for help in this little operation. With money like that, the man thought, he could build his own museum. He would build it somewhere where it was warm. Then he would be in charge. He would make the decisions.

He walked past the reassembled *Utahraptor*. The huge skeleton towered menacingly over the man. Well, the man knew he had done as much as he could with that thing. Now it was onto something more important.

He walked over to the display case that held the claw. Around him the stillness of the raptor exhibits almost unnerved him. He was very glad they were only fossils and reconstructions. But, as he raised his crowbar to smash it down on the case, he froze in sudden terror. The room was filled with a terrible wailing cry.

The man whirled around, raising his crowbar to defend himself, but there was no one there. Then the strange wail broke out again. It rose and fell with an unearthly sound. It seemed to be coming from everywhere at once. For one dreadful moment the man thought maybe the cry was coming from the *Utahraptor* itself!

The man's nerve broke. He ran for the door.

In his panic he never realized the door was slightly ajar. He went tearing through, tripped over Dakota's foot that was thoughtfully placed in his path, and landed hard on the ground. All the breath was knocked out of him. His crowbar skittered from his grasp. A bright light flashed in his face further disorienting him. Someone landed on his back in a flying tackle, twisting his arms behind him so he couldn't get up. He was caught.

"Oh no," said the distressed voice of Shelly Brooks as she shone her flashlight in the man's face. It was a face that was mostly covered by a large black beard. "Dakota, it's Bob, the maintenance chief!"

"I know," said Dakota, but there was no mistake. They had their vandal. Dakota stepped to the bars on the nearest window and grabbed hold.

CHAPTER THIRTY-TWO

GREED

Detective Franks and PaleoJoe and about a hundred policemen stormed up the stairway to the second floor of the Balboa. They had been hiding in the Tombs waiting for a signal from Bob who was left on duty with the main night security officer. He was supposed to notify them at once if anything should look suspicious. Detective Franks had it figured that the vandal would strike again. He wanted to catch him in the act.

When the alarms began to ring, Detective Franks wasted no time in leading the charge to the Special Exhibits room. As they stormed up to the Raptor Room they were greeted by the sight of Cleveland sitting on the back of Bob, and Shelly shining her flashlight in the poor man's face. But Detective Franks was quick to spot the crowbar on the floor. He put two and two together.

"Bob?" PaleoJoe looked distressed. "Why did you do it?"

"Buzzsaw was going to give me enough money so that I could have my own museum," said Bob gruffly, as police officers handcuffed him. "I didn't like to do it, PaleoJoe, but it was an awful lot of money."

PaleoJoe watched as Detective Franks' officers led Bob away. He sighed.

"Ignorance and greed," said Cleveland thoughtfully.

"What?" asked Shelly.

"My dad always says that the two worst enemies of the human race are ignorance and greed," said Cleveland.

"Yes," agreed Shelly. "I suppose that's right."

"Well Bob sure got nailed by the greed thing," said Dakota.

"I knew Bob and Buzzsaw had been friends," said PaleoJoe. "They knew each other when Buzzsaw worked here. I had forgotten about it."

Shelly felt badly. Bob had been the Question Asker at the door to the Tombs. He had been her friend. But she understood that he had been Buzzsaw's friend, too.

"So how did you do it, Miss Shelly Brooks," asked PaleoJoe trying to shake off the gloom left

173

from Bob's betrayal.

"It was Dakota's idea," said Shelly.

"Well, Sir?" Detective Franks flipped out his notebook to make it official while Dakota reported.

"Shelly figured out how we could hide in the museum," said Dakota.

PaleoJoe cleared his throat and did his one eyebrow thing at Shelly. Shelly frowned. Was this what it felt like to be nefarious? Then she shrugged her shoulders.

"Dakota is a bad influence on me," she said sweetly. It had, after all, been an adventure.

"Peachy," said Dakota. "So then, we hid in the *Megatherium*. Cleveland saw Bob go into the Raptor Room with the crowbar and so we went into action. I remembered that Shelly had recorded the coyotes howling when we were in Utah. I thought about Barnabus Johnson and the curse and we just sort of played her recording into the room. I guess Bob's imagination did the rest."

"Yes," said PaleoJoe sadly. "Buzzsaw owes a big debt on that one as far as I'm concerned."

"We'll catch him someday," said Shelly. "Dakota and I will help you."

"Sure," said Dakota. "You can count on the Dinosaur Detective Club to bring in the bad guys!"

174

CHAPTER THIRTY-THREE

THE TOMBS ONCE AGAIN

In the morning the Balboa was a very busy place. Crowds of people showed up to see if the Raptor Room would really open or not and to hopefully discover more about the curse. They were all very pleased to find the Exhibit open. The follow-ups in the newspapers made much of Cleveland's fossil. June Pierceson, herself, gave him an interview in which she treated Cleveland very politely and said a lot of good things about him.

Before he returned home, Cleveland gave Dakota a gift of a brand new pair of sunglasses with both highly reflective lens firmly glued into place. When Dakota put them on, even Shelly had to admit that, he looked dangerous.

"Thanks for everything," said Cleveland when

he said good-bye. "Come and visit me soon and we'll go white water kayaking!"

It was a few days after the departure of Cleveland that Dakota found himself meeting Shelly on the steps of the Balboa. They had received a call from PaleoJoe who wanted them to come and see him in the Tombs.

The day was cloudy and an approaching thunderstorm grumbled in the distance. Shelly was waiting for Dakota on the front steps to the museum. She was looking sort of glum.

"How can we go into the Tombs," she asked, "when there won't be anyone there to ask us the Explorer's Question?"

Dakota shrugged. "I don't know," he said. "But come on. PaleoJoe is waiting for us."

They entered the Balboa together stopping for a minute to admire the Raptor banner still suspended from the balcony.

"It's a very cool exhibit," said Shelly.

"I'm glad the Dinosaur Detective Club was able to help PaleoJoe," said Dakota.

As they stood at the top of the squeaky stairs, a loud rumble of thunder announced the arrival of the storm. Neither one of them felt like dancing and jumping down the musical stairs in their usual way. So they simply walked down.

At the bottom the door to the Tombs was shut and when Dakota tried it, he found it was locked.

"Well?" he said looking at Shelly.

Shelly shrugged her shoulders. "I guess you could try."

So Dakota rapped out their secret coded knock. *Rap-a tat-a-tattat-rap-rap.*

For a minute, nothing happened.

Then, slowly, the door opened.

"*Mmeerow,*" said the brown and white whiskered face that peeked out.

"Saber?" Dakota couldn't believe it. "Saber? Is that you?"

And of course it was. Saber trotted out to prove it to his friend, the boy who liked to stuff him into bags. He rolled over on his side and invited Dakota to pet his creamy striped tummy. Which of course Dakota did. Shelly helped, too. Saber began to purr.

"Who dares to seek admittance to the Tombs?" From the open door the voice boomed out, not as deep and menacing as Bob's, and full of laughter.

Shelly looked up. Mike, dressed in blue coveralls just a bit too big for her, leaned in the doorway.

"Mike, it's you!" Shelly squeaked.

"Last time I looked it was," said Mike her face wrinkling into a smile. "Are you ready to answer the Explorer's Question? Only the bravest and the smartest are allowed to enter the Tombs, you know."

"Yes! Ready!" answered Shelly and Dakota together.

"Good," said Mike. "And the sooner the better too because I need some help polishing these floors and then there are about two dozen lights that need changing, not to mention dusting in the Raptor Room. I could use some help."

Dakota scooped up Saber and set the small purring cat on his shoulders.

"We're ready when you are," he said happily.

The End

About PaleoJoe

PaleoJoe is a real paleontologist whose recent adventures included digging in the famous Como Bluff for Allosaurus, Camptosaurus, and Apatosaurus. A graduate of Niagara University, just outside of the fossil rich Niagara Falls and Lewiston area of New York, Joseph has collected fossils since he was 10 years old. He has gone on digs around the United States and abroad, hunting for dinosaur fossils with some of the most famous and respected paleontologists in the world. He is a member of the Paleontological Research Institute and Society of Vertebrate Paleontology and is the winner of the prestigious Katherine Palmer Award for his work communicating dinosaur and fossil information with children and communities. He has given over 300 school presentations around the country.

He is also the author of *The Complete Guide to Michigan Fossils* and *Hidden Dinosaurs*.

About Wendy Caszatt-Allen

Wendy Caszatt-Allen is a teacher, poet, and playwright. She teaches 8th grade language arts in the Mid-Prairie Community School District in Iowa. A graduate of Interlochen in 1980, and of Michigan State in 1984, she went on to complete an MA at the University of Iowa. She is currently working on a Ph.D. in Language, Literacy, and Culture at the same institution. Recently her poetry has appeared in the Dunes Review. In addition, several of her plays for middle school players have been produced and performed on stage as well as appearing on local television. She has given presentations at the Iowa Council of Teachers of English and Language Arts and at the National Council of Teachers of English on reading and writing with adolescents.

She has released *Adventures of Pachelot: Last Voyage of the Griffon* and will be releasing *Fort Brokenheart* in 2007 with Mackinac Island Press.